P9-EJU-286

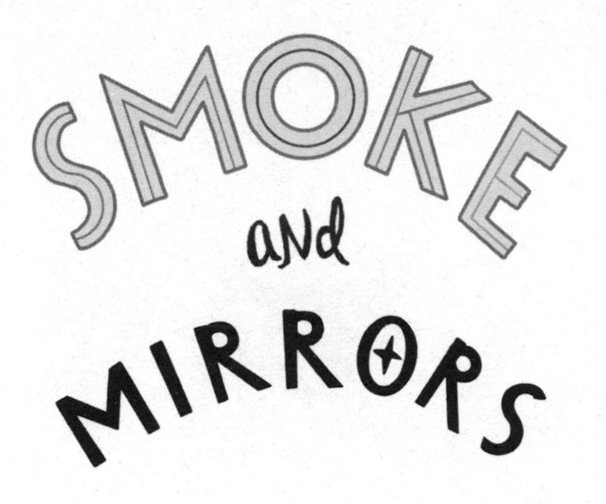
SMOKE
and
MIRRORS

A Paula Wiseman Book
Simon & Schuster Books for Young Readers
New York London Toronto
Sydney New Delhi

SIMON & SCHUSTER BOOKS FOR YOUNG READERS
An imprint of Simon & Schuster Children's Publishing Division
1230 Avenue of the Americas, New York, New York 10020

For information about special discounts for bulk purchases, please contact Simon & Schuster Special Sales at 1-866-506-1949 or business@simonandschuster.com.
The Simon & Schuster Speakers Bureau can bring authors to your live event. For more information or to book an event, contact the Simon & Schuster Speakers Bureau at 1-866-248-3049 or visit our website at www.simonspeakers.com.
Jacket design by Chloë Foglia
Interior design by Tom Daly
The text for this book is set in ITC New Baskerville.
The illustrations for this book were rendered in pen and ink and digitally.
Manufactured in the United States of America
0818 FFG
First Edition
2 4 6 8 10 9 7 5 3 1
Library of Congress Cataloging-in-Publication Data
Names: Halbrook, Kristin, author.
Title: Smoke and mirrors / K.D. Halbrook.
Description: First edition. | New York : Simon & Schuster Books for Young Readers, [2018]. | Summary: Bullied while attending fifth grade with the Islanders, Sasha, who always loved being part of Cirque Magnifique, wishes it would all go away but when her parents disappear in the Smoke, it is up to her to save them.
Identifiers: LCCN 2018000433 | ISBN 9781534405042 (hardback) | ISBN 9781534405066 (eBook)
Subjects: | CYAC: Fantasy. | Circus—Fiction. | Magic—Fiction. | Missing persons—Fiction. | Bullying—Fiction. | Schools—Fiction. | BISAC: JUVENILE FICTION / Fantasy & Magic. | JUVENILE FICTION / Performing Arts / Circus. | JUVENILE FICTION / Family / General (see also headings under Social Issues).
Classification: LCC PZ7.H12837 Smo 2018 | DDC [Fic]—dc23
LC record available at https://lccn.loc.gov/2018000433

To my Pixies, who give me joy to mirror

THE EDGE OF THE WORLD

The Magician could call a flock of birds from a top hat. He could make a baby elephant float off the ground with a wave of his wand. He could disappear in a plume of Smoke.

But his favorite trick was making other people disappear in a plume of Smoke.

The Magician stood at the shore of the sea at the Edge of the World and watched the far-off ripples of water. After a time a grand, black-and-white creature broke the surface, then disappeared under the waves again. One blink, and the Magician would have missed it.

He held his breath. Stepped into the water. Waited.

The rippling waves rose, pushing the Magician back from the sea.

The foam that lapped the sand berated him. *No,* the water seemed to say. *Away.*

The Magician curled his lip and turned to face the Forest of Thorny Trees again. He raised his fingers, and swathes of Smoke lifted from the ground as though they were puppets being forced up by their strings.

The Magician walked through the Smoke. He turned his thoughts away from the sea and to another place. A colorful, happy dot on a faraway island. His sneer grew. But then . . .

He stopped walking.

The Magician's kind of magic could never tell the future or read minds, but for the first time in a long time, the Magician had a *feeling*. A deliciously dark one. Something was going to happen at Cirque Magnifique.

The Magician pulled more Smoke from the earth, gathered it into his palm, and blew it across the sea.

His sneer stretched into a cruel smile.

CHAPTER 1

Sasha's father flew like a bird.

His hair was as black as night and slicked back, with a shine like the moon glinting off a smooth, obsidian beach stone. His body and arms and legs were black too, his long, skinny limbs wrapped in his night-colored bodysuit, with only two white stripes on his shoulders. His hands, only slightly less dark than his bodysuit, flexed in anticipation. He stood tall on the platform, so that it seemed he could reach the highest branches in an old cedar tree, but really all he held on to with his talon hands was the bar high, high overhead.

"Watch this, Sasha!" he called down.

Sasha looked up from her book, leaving her finger pressed against the last word she'd read. She stood with the ruby-red tent as the backdrop and watched her father leap from his nest, soar across the sky, release the bar, and fling himself into a triple twist. Sasha's heart thumped painfully as her father emerged from his pretzel, too slowly it seemed, so that she gasped and cried out. Her book fell to the dirt-and-sawdust ground.

"Dad!"

But just as Sasha thought he'd fall into the thick mat below the trapeze, he sprung open like a flower desperate for sun and reached for the bar Mr. Ticklefar had pushed toward him. Her father's claws grasped and curled, and he soared to the opposite platform while Sasha caught her breath and tried to slow her racing pulse. His teeth gleamed as he grinned down at her.

"Little Chick," her dad said from his perch. "Do you like the new trick? Won't it wow the audience?"

"I think it's scary."

"That's not so scary. You know what's scary? Opening yourself up to others to love with all your heart. But it's the most wonderful thing too." Sasha sighed and rolled her eyes, but Dad grinned. "Get changed and we'll practice. Once we have it perfected, I plan to do it without a net."

Sasha retrieved her book, forced a smile, and waved up at him. If his new trick frightened her, it would terrify the audience in that good, tingling way that made relief the most beautiful emotion of all.

In a moment Sasha's mother stood next to Sasha. Her plumage was different from Sasha's dad's: an assortment of tropical colors beaded and sparkling on her leotard, and two slim, long, pale legs poking out below. On the weekend Sasha's mother would wear a headpiece even more elaborate than the leotard, and weighing almost as much as her entire body, as she worked and twisted the rainbow of ribbons that dropped from the ceiling of the tent.

"Did you catch the timing?" Sasha's mother asked, pressing a finger to her daughter's elbow. Sasha's muscles relaxed, and she smiled, for real this time.

Sasha dog-eared the corner of the page she had been reading and set her book on the bottom step of the stands. "Looks easy. Throw when his shoulders are highest during the second twist."

"Right. Are you sure you don't want me to show you up on the platform?"

Sasha shook her head. "I got it. I don't need help."

Her mom plopped a kiss onto the top of Sasha's head. "You always say that. And you're usually right. My very capable girl."

Sasha changed and climbed the ladder to the aerial platform, high in the big tent sky. When Sasha was on the platform, she felt gigantic. Strong. So tall that nothing could hurt her. Now the stands were empty, but on the weekends they filled so that everyone in the audience sat shoulder to shoulder, packed into every space. All those people watching her . . . silent and waiting . . . sent tingles up Sasha's back. And when they applauded after she and Dad completed their tricks, she felt like royalty. A Cirque princess. But she knew that earning their admiration took lots of practice. So she held the bar, counting beats in her head to get the timing perfect. Far below, Mom waved and grinned at Sasha.

"You can do it!"

Dad waited on the platform opposite Sasha. Somewhere in the tent Aunt Chanteuse began to sing. Her songs were at times melancholy, pulling surprise tears from the audience, but at other times jovial and uplifting. That was how she sang now, trilling until her notes sounded more like laughter than music. Aunt Chanteuse could pull extra rainbows from the gossamer bubbles that floated around the tent as she sang, just as Madame Mermadia could turn plain old dust motes into dazzling, dancing fairies with a toss of her red hair. Just as Mom could send the sweetest, softest breezes throughout the tent as she twirled on the silk ribbons, and how Dad could turn a drumbeat into a bolt of lightning in the audience's hearts. This was the magic of the Cirque, and Sasha loved being surrounded by it.

"Sashaaaaa, toss the baaarrrr," Aunt Chanteuse sang into the upper reaches of the tent. Dad laughed, and Sasha couldn't help but laugh too. She shook herself awake.

"Okay, I'm ready!" she shouted, pulling her arms back.

"That's my amazing girl," Dad called over.

All through their practice, Sasha hurled the bar, learning the timing perfectly. Her parents applauded. Aunt Chanteuse sang. Mr. Ticklefar, the short ringmaster with the curled-ends mustache, tipped his hat and said, "Aha!" and "Well done!" Sasha filled, filled, filled with joy until she thought she would burst like a confetti cannon, spilling a rainbow of plastic-wrapped candies everywhere.

When the dinner bell rang, Sasha scrambled down the platform ladder. Mom helped her leap the last few steps, catching Sasha in her arms and laughing. There was always so much laughter at the Cirque. Some nights, as friends gathered in the cottages to tell stories—Mr. Ticklefar was the best, his stories of far-off travels told with the most ridiculous facial expressions—Sasha would have to hold her aching belly and gasp for breath for all the giggling everyone did.

Toddy, Sasha's little brother, emerged from one of his many secret hiding places under the audience bleachers and took Sasha's hand. The family walked to the dining tent together, followed closely by Mr.

Ticklefar and Aunt Chanteuse. Along the way they caught up with Madame Mermadia and her children, Shelby and Griffin. They were all halfway through costume fittings, trailing strands of sequins behind them.

"Your arm's falling off." Sasha pointed at the length of fabric hanging from Shelby's shoulder. Shelby was five years older than Sasha, and this was the first year Shelby would join her mom in the Magical Mermaid Lagoon performance.

"It feels like both of them are," Shelby said. "My mom's making me do strength training in the water tank. I hope there's something good for dinner. I'm hungry enough to eat an elephant."

"You look like an elephant," teased Griffin, Shelby's twin brother. Shelby reached for him, and Griffin bolted across the field to the dining tent, shrieking as Shelby chased after him.

"They're getting so big," Mom said, same as she did every time she saw Shelby and Griffin.

"They're not the only ones." Madam Mermadia tousled Sasha's hair. "Are you excited about your first day of school tomorrow?"

Mr. Ticklefar, overhearing Madam Mermadia's question, stepped forward. "She will astound them all!"

"It will be deeeliiightfulll," Aunt Chanteuse sang.

But Sasha's heart pounded harder than it had when

she'd watched Dad do his new trick for the first time. Even though she was going into fifth grade, Sasha had never before stepped foot in a public school. She and Toddy had always been taught at the Cirque, learning their letters and numbers, as well as the lore of the Cirque; practicing science experiments in between helping Mr. Ticklefar take apart and repair machines; and almost always—for Sasha, at least—getting caught up in the fantastical worlds of her favorite books. But school would be different. She wouldn't have Mr. Ticklefar's stories to teach her geography, or Madame Mermadia's lessons on oceanography. Would there be any magic at school at all?

Mr. Ticklefar always said the Cirque was the best place on earth, but there were important and useful things to learn in other places and from other people. Sasha's parents agreed, and so she and Toddy were to start a new adventure in their education.

Sasha put on a brave face and talked bigger than she felt to Madame Mermadia. "It'll be great."

Sasha squeezed Toddy's hand. The siblings shared a secret look and reluctantly smiled. It was good, Sasha thought. Having a brother. Taking these next steps with someone familiar by her side. Even if every moment at school was not-great, Sasha and Toddy would have each other.

CHAPTER 2

After the dinner plates were licked clean and the berry cobbler was being passed around, Mr. Ticklefar climbed atop a table and cleared his throat. As Cirque Magnifique's ringmaster, he was the unofficial cataloger of Cirque lore and traditions.

"And now it is time for a story." For such a small man, he had a voice that could soar over hundreds of people. "I always tell of a great adventure when our wee ones go off to school for the first time. There is much to be taught here, but there is much to learn from the Islanders, too, and so we send our children to their schools after a time. But it's important that our children never forget where they come from, nor forget that there is a new adventure around every corner. Even if that corner is only the other side of the island. Tonight I shall tell the story of . . ." Mr. Ticklefar waved his arms around as though he were searching the air for inspiration. "'The Weasel and the Riddle'!"

A stifled groan came from Sasha's left. Griffin rolled his eyes at her.

"Not this dumb story again." The whole Cirque had heard the story "The Weasel and the Riddle" before. They had heard all of Mr. Ticklefar's stories many times; they clamored for the telling of them over and over again.

"You don't like it?" Sasha said.

Griffin shrugged. "It's a good story. But he pretends it's all real. Like it happened."

A sudden chill made Sasha shudder. This was the first time she'd ever heard someone from the Cirque voice doubt over their lore. She leaned in close to Griffin so that no one else could hear her. "Mr. Ticklefar's adventure did happen. Why don't you believe him?"

"You would believe anything he says," Griffin said. "With your mom and all. But the stories are all just fairy tales. I mean, I like them. It creeps out the Islanders whenever I tell 'The Weasel and the Riddle' to them. What if they got caught and couldn't answer the riddle correctly? But it's not *real.* There's no such thing as a Sharp-Beaked Weasel. And the other stories

Mr. Ticklefar tells, like the ones about the Magician? They're pretend. No one can do magic like—"

"Shh!" Shelby elbowed Griffin. "Don't listen to him," she said to Sasha. "He talks more like an Islander every day. Thinks just because you can't see a thing that it's not real. But we know what's real, huh, Sasha?"

Sasha looked at her little brother. She looked at her parents, holding hands across the table. She saw things. Lots of things. And they were all real.

Mr. Ticklefar began his story. "There was once an ancient forest made of thorny, stern-gray trees that could never grow leaves. The forest was desolate and lonely, and few creatures lived in it. The Sharp-Beaked Weasel, however, called it home."

"See?" Griffin said. "Trees that can't grow leaves? That's not how science works. They have to make chloro—"

"Quiet!" Shelby whispered.

Griffin scowled. "Only babies believe this stuff. If the kids at school find out you think the stories are real, they'll laugh at you."

"I'm ten minutes older than you, and I believe it, so what does that make you?" Shelby stuck her tongue out at her brother, then turned to Sasha. "Ignore Griffin. He's just winding you up because you're starting school for the first time tomorrow. School is fine. It's good to go and learn things they don't teach at the Cirque. The Islanders can be a little . . ." Shelby shrugged without finishing her thought.

Islanders could be . . . what? Sasha didn't like that mysterious missing word. But before she could ask for more details, Mr. Ticklefar's voice rose dramatically.

"Had I not been distracted by the strange gray sap dripping down that tree, he'd never have snuck up on me! Well, there I was, nearly squeezed to death by that weasel's strong tail. A mighty fine dinner I would be! And my hat for dessert. Or so he thought. 'I challenge you to a riddle,' I bellowed, with what little breath I had left. You see"—Mr. Ticklefar's voice lowered—"I knew that some fantastical creatures *must* accept a riddle challenge. I wasn't sure that would be true for the weasel, but I had to try. And to my great luck, it worked!"

"Talking weasels," Griffin muttered.

"*Riddling* weasels," Shelby said triumphantly.

"So that rascally weasel finished telling me his riddle," Mr. Ticklefar continued. "I said to him: 'You must loosen your grip if I'm to think.' He did, knowing I wouldn't run. That would be against the rules of riddling. 'Bitter and sweet,' that weasel had said. 'And once tasted, lost forever.' Those fantastical creatures like to make riddles of love, but in this case it didn't work, for once tasted, love stayed with you always." Mr. Ticklefar's voice boomed. "I was tangled up with that weasel for three suns up, and three suns down! I was mighty tired. And hungry! If the weasel was half as hungry as I was, then he was sure to gobble me in one great bite if I answered wrong. I could have eaten just about anything, but what I truly longed for was . . ." Mr. Ticklefar paused dramatically. Everyone in the dining hall was on the edge of their seats, even though they knew how the story ended. "Well, I longed for the very thing that was the answer to the riddle: chocolate!"

The dining hall erupted in giggles. As Mr. Ticklefar detailed the weasel's angry fit at being defeated, Toddy let out a long, slow breath. Sasha took his hand and squeezed.

"The story's true, isn't it?" she whispered to him.

He nodded, resolute. One of Sasha's favorite things about her brother was that he was always so steady, so sure. If Griffin's words made Sasha question the lore of the Cirque, Toddy's unwavering belief steadied her questioning mind again.

Everyone applauded. The tale was finished. The ringmaster looked over at Sasha and Toddy. "Things are changing, wee ones. Remember that you are brave enough and smart enough to succeed in all the adventures you have."

Mr. Ticklefar took his seat again while Aunt

Chanteuse led them all in merry songs. There was dancing and laughter until Toddy fell asleep on Sasha's shoulder, cuddling his favorite rainbow-moose stuffed animal, and even Sasha's eyes started to get heavy and drooping.

"Off to bed with you two," Mom said.

Dad hoisted Sasha and Toddy both in one great heave, and strolled to their cottage, the sounds of the dining tent fading little by little until all that was left was a gentle ringing in Sasha's ears, the memory of story and song and dance.

"Will school be as fun as the Cirque?" Sasha rubbed her eyes against sleep. Her body was tired, but her mind buzzed with nerves.

"It will be a different kind of fun," Mom said. "And you'll make new friends and get to read new books, too. . . . But also—" Mom crouched down so she was eye-to-eye with Sasha. "I know you are always the very best big sister anyone could hope for," Mom whispered, gently taking Sasha's hands in hers. "But you'll have to be an especially wonderful big sister at school. All the Cirque knows that Toddy doesn't talk much, and we all adjust for his needs and no one thinks much of it. But at school . . . it's possible people won't be so patient with Toddy. Won't understand him. You'll help, though, won't you?"

"I don't have to. Toddy's magic. They'll see it," Sasha said.

Mom searched Sasha's face. Her eyes were soft as she said, "How can they not?"

Sasha smiled at that and climbed into bed, next to Toddy. When she closed her eyes, her dreams tugged at her to come and play through the night.

In the morning the tender sun beckoned to them through pink smudged skies. Their Cirque friends and family paused their work and rehearsals and waved good-bye. Sasha and Toddy strode through the knee-high grasses that grew on either side of the dirt path to the bus stop, until the hems of their clothes were wet. It was always like that on the island. Misty and damp and the kind of green that wasn't sure if it really wanted to be gray.

Shelby and Griffin saw Sasha and Toddy coming and waved for them to run.

"Hurry!" Shelby called. "If you're late, Mr. Orner will be the crankiest bus driver you've ever seen."

The older Cirque kids caught a different bus to their secondary school, but all Cirque kids caught the bus at the same stop. Down the road, the larger bus that would carry Sasha and Toddy to the elementary school was cresting the hill that unofficially marked the beginning of the Cirque half of the island. Sasha squeezed Toddy's hand. They broke into a sprint, and reached the stop just as the bus was opening its doors.

"Five minutes early," the bus driver growled. "That's what time you're supposed to be here."

A knot lodged in Sasha's throat. She froze, staring at Mr. Orner's square, stony face. Her feet would not move. Last night's songs, playing on repeat in Sasha's mind all morning, screeched to a halt. Heavy silence bore down on her.

"You getting on?" the bus driver asked. His fingers tapped the steering wheel impatiently. "I heard your brother don't talk. Didn't hear that about you, though. But you Cirque kids are all strange."

A dozen replies dashed across Sasha's tongue. Her brother could talk . . . to her, at least. And so could she! And Cirque kids weren't strange. What a mean thing for an adult to say. But the freezing feeling spread to Sasha's mouth, and when she opened her lips, nothing came out.

The bus driver squinted. "I can't wait all morning. Get on or go back," he said.

Sasha looked at the bus windows. All the kids were watching her. Some pointed and some laughed. Some just stared. Heat flared into Sasha's cheeks and thawed her out.

"Sorry," she mumbled, taking the first step onto the bus.

Sasha scanned the seats. The only open row was three from the back, the row right in front of two boys with draping arms and sly smiles. They gave Sasha that chilly feeling again, the way they watched her without ever looking away. Any seat on the bus would have been better than the ones in that row.

But if the Cirque had taught Sasha anything, it was that she was strong. She grabbed Toddy's hand behind her, marched to the row, and sat with her back straight and chin held high. The bus's doors closed, and the big machine rolled away from the Cirque. Sasha watched the flags fluttering in the morning breeze until they were completely out of sight over the hill.

That's when one of the boys tugged on Sasha's hair. At first it was a soft pull, so gentle that Sasha couldn't decide if it had actually happened. Perhaps it had just been the way the bus had bounced over the gravel road, with its trenches and potholes. *Why*, after all, would someone pull her hair? No one at the Cirque did that. Sasha turned and looked at the boys behind her. They stared out the window as though nothing were happening.

"Stop it, please."

One boy looked at her. "Stop what?"

Sasha's face went hot. She had accused the boys of something they hadn't done.

"Nothing. Never mind." Sasha faced front again. But then another tug, and another. Harder each time. It wasn't the pitted road, and it wasn't her imagination. Sasha leaned a bit forward and ignored the tugs, her belly beginning to simmer with something foul and acidic. She would have held her temper all the way to school, though, if they had only been messing with her. But then they flicked the back of Toddy's head.

"Stop it!" Sasha stood and spun her body, fury blazing in her eyes. No one hurt her brother. The boys threw their hands into the air as if to say *Not us* and laughed. Sasha jammed her fists into her hips. "I know you're doing that!"

"Sit down, girl!" the bus driver called over his shoulder.

Sasha fell into her seat and draped her arm over Toddy's head to protect him. After a few minutes her muscles began to burn, but she held on. She stared out the window, swallowing back the gross taste in her throat and battling tears. Mom had said school would be fun. She'd said there would be new friends to be made. Sasha didn't understand what was happening. Maybe the bus ride was the worst of it all and as soon as Sasha got to the school campus, things would be different.

"Hey, freaks." In the back seat of the bus, another boy spoke up. He'd been quiet up to this point, watching carefully, not joining the teasing. But now he leaned forward slightly and spoke, so low that only the kids in the nearby rows could hear him. Sasha heard him loud and clear, but she refused to acknowledge him, her still body sweltering with embarrassment and frustration.

One of the boys behind her tugged her hair again. "Hey, Kirk's talking to you, freak."

Sasha wasn't a freak, and neither was Toddy. She gazed around the bus, hoping just one other kid would speak up and defend them. This was a new world for Sasha, and she needed someone to show her how to navigate it.

The only person who caught Sasha's eye was a girl with long, slinky hair and round cheeks. She looked nice, and for a moment Sasha's chest hollowed out with hope. Perhaps that girl would say something. She would be the friend Mom and Dad were talking about. The girl took in a breath, her eyes flicked to Kirk, and whatever it was that silently passed between them made the girl's gaze fall to the floor and her shoulders slump. Instead of helping Sasha, she turned to face the front of the bus again.

"You're ugly," that voice said.

Sasha had always liked her dark, unruly hair and wide gray eyes, and even though she was thin enough to make her knees a bit knobby, she was also strong. No one had ever called her ugly before.

"What's your name?" Kirk asked.

"Sasha."

"Sausage?" The boys laughed.

"I said Sasha!"

"Sausage, it is."

When the bus finally reached the school, Sasha's scalp ached and her eyes itched from all the tears she held back. She turned in her seat to look at Kirk. The boy had thick brown hair and big green eyes that Sasha would have liked if he hadn't been so mean. Kirk stuck his tongue out at her, and Sasha quickly turned forward again, her stomach aching at the very bottom.

CHAPTER 3

And so it went every morning for several weeks. Pebble after pebble after pebble dropped into Sasha's stomach until it became difficult to lug her heavy body around. Mom and Dad had to entice her out of bed in the mornings with elaborate breakfasts in the cottage and long speeches about how things would get more fun at school soon.

It was only Toddy who could really get her moving.

"I want to go to school, but I don't want to go alone," he said to her. "It will be okay."

And so Sasha hauled herself out the door, her step becoming lighter as they traipsed to the bus stop. Perhaps this was the day, she always thought, that Jenny

Myers, the girl with the slinky hair, would finally want to be her friend.

After all, there wasn't anything wrong with being a Cirque kid. Sasha knew that, even if the other kids weren't so sure. The Cirque kids were color in a gray world, they were many languages and strange accents, they were the children of bizarre grown-ups who didn't have normal jobs or wear normal clothes or carry the same tired expressions in their eyes, like the other island parents did.

Cirque kids were different.

"The Islanders just don't understand us," Shelby said one morning, gathering Sasha into a hug. "They don't know about magic or transformations or . . . Smoke." Shelby shuddered.

For it was the way of the Smoke to haunt Cirque Magnifique, rising out of the ground when it thought no one was looking. Sasha had never seen with her own eyes the terrible things the Smoke was capable of, and no one talked about it in the open, but she had overheard whispers when the Cirque folk hadn't known she was listening. Broken tales about months of dark rains so that the hillsides became waterfalls and no one could come to see performances, about tents going up in sudden flames, and the scariest tale of all, the one about

Cirque folks mysteriously going missing before their time, as though the Smoke opened its gaping maws and swallowed them whole.

That was why it was so important for the Cirque to have Lights. They were the people who wandered onto the grounds, hardly knowing why they came, only knowing they had to join the crew. Lights were the ones who walked with beauty, who had a way of deflecting the Smoke's terrible deeds back onto itself, shaming it underground and keeping the Cirque safe. And so it was, twelve years ago, when Sasha and Toddy's mom had wandered into Cirque Magnifique at the stroke of midnight, knowing it was her destiny to be there.

At least that was the story Sasha and Toddy's father told whenever the night turned a certain way, when shadows lengthened into particular, spiny shapes, when the taste in the air turned bitter as Sasha stuck out her tongue to meet it. When Toddy clung even tighter to his fantastical-creature stuffed animals. These were the nights when, instead of choosing to fear the fog that rolled in like waves on a beach, they welcomed Mr. Ticklefar and Aunt Chanteuse to their cottage for tea and pastries and talked about love.

"Your mother was eighteen," the story went. "And the most beautiful woman I'd ever seen. Her light was like an aura. It followed her around. When she smiled, it beamed across the whole village. She said to us all, 'I have been called to this place and I don't know why.' And then she laughed, and true as anything, fairies rose from the grasses and their wings glittered in the night."

Sasha and Toddy always loved that part of the story best. They both knew that if they woke at just the right time on the night of the full moon, they too would see those fairies.

"Well," Dad would go on. "We all knew why she'd come. Our last Light had left the island and paddled into the sea as an otter—it had simply been the end of his time—and we were waiting for a new Light to be revealed. You never know how a Light will arrive. Sometimes it blossoms out of someone already part of the Cirque. Other times it arrives in the form of a stranger. That's how your mom came to us. I loved her immediately—"

"I'm certain I loved you even before that," Mom would cut in. "So tall and bold, and that smile with enough room to welcome everyone."

Dad would take Mom's hand. Then Sasha and Toddy always rolled their eyes at each other.

"Lucky me, she loved me back. Love always makes us better than we were before. It makes Lights of us all."

Sasha had always believed that. She, too, had a little bit of the Light about her, as surrounded by love as she was. But the kids on the other side of the island didn't understand the Cirque, they didn't understand Light, and they certainly didn't understand Sasha or Toddy.

Which is why, after weeks of name-calling and hair-pulling, Sasha stopped smiling. She read more and more books, trying to turn her real world into something like the fantasies between those pages. She forgot that her life used to be a bubbling well of magic. All the sparkles and sequins that used to reflect in Sasha's eyes turned dull. She ran her hands over costumes and frowned. The embellishments were nothing more than tiny pieces of tin and plastic. Mr. Ticklefar's stories became harder and harder to believe, and even Aunt Chanteuse's songs couldn't lift Sasha's spirits. The only thing that made Sasha feel better was being around Toddy. His bright eyes and ready grin always left Sasha believing she could float again.

Sometimes Sasha wished Toddy's magic worked on the Islanders, too.

CHAPTER 4

As time passed, Sasha grew used to the way adults at school furrowed their eyebrows and other kids pulled faces when Toddy refused to speak. It was highly unlikely that Toddy's teacher, Mrs. Flint, knew anything about magic, so it was no surprise Toddy wouldn't talk to her.

Toddy would often slip out of his own classroom when no one was looking and tiptoe into Sasha's. He loved the big windows there, the colorful posters on the walls, and the scrubby turtle in the tank next to the sink.

It would take only moments for Mrs. Flint to come wheezing into Sasha's classroom, her hand pressed over her heart, trying to catch her breath. She'd lift her finger and point at Toddy with narrowed, beady eyes.

"I know you understand what I'm saying, young

man," she'd say. "You get outta that seat now and get back to your own classroom."

Toddy would turn to Sasha and grasp her hand, folding his fingers in hers. Sasha would squeeze Toddy's hand back and glare at Mrs. Flint.

"Toddy doesn't want to go with you. He needs a smarter teacher."

Mrs. Flint was not the kind of woman who liked being talked back to. Her own children, though they were full-grown adults, never attempted that death-defying deed. The other teachers let her have her own way. And even Mr. Rottenhammer, the school principal, avoided Mrs. Flint at all costs.

"That boy don't speak, you little troublemaker. Don't you go making up stories. Know what that makes you? A liar. Nobody likes liars. Nobody. Know what liars deserve? A walloping on their behind. If I could do it, I would."

But Sasha was the one person at that school who never seemed to have her feathers ruffled by Mrs. Flint. Nobody knew exactly how Sasha stayed so calm, despite Mrs. Flint's thunderstorm face, but she did. The general consensus was that Sasha was too stupid to know that Mrs. Flint was angry at her.

"Making up stories doesn't make me a liar," Sasha always said, still holding tight to her brother. She thought of Mr. Ticklefar and his wild tales and how happy they made everyone at the Cirque. "It makes me a storyteller."

"How dare you speak to me that way?" Mrs. Flint's voice always rose louder and higher with every word she spoke. Her cheeks would turn pink, then red, then nearly purple, and her chest would plump out as though she were hiding a goose under her shirt. "Like you're better than what you are . . . one of those sparkly freaks. I've a mind to call your mother and have her pick you both up, only she never takes anything I say to heart. Pompous! That's what you all are." Before Mrs. Flint could grasp Toddy at the elbow with her red nails and drag him kicking and screaming away, Sasha always pressed a gentle kiss to his cheek.

"I'll see you after school," she'd promise.

Sasha would squint at Mrs. Flint's retreating form. Why couldn't the woman see that Toddy was full of magic? He was special. And Sasha, as everyone on this side of the island liked to remind her, was nothing.

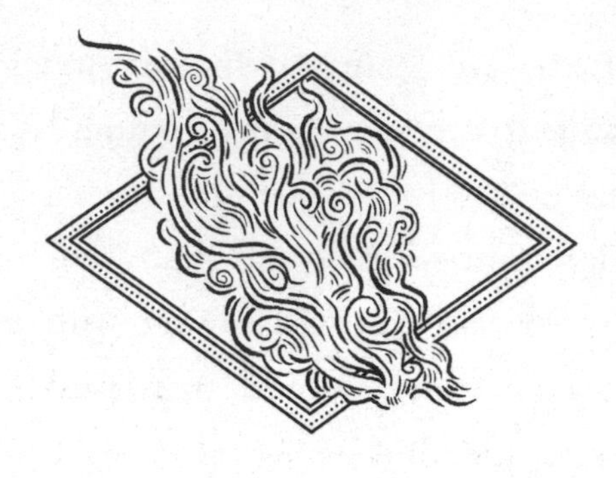

CHAPTER 5

On an afternoon in mid-October, Sasha's mom picked her up from the bus stop.

"How was school?"

"Toddy's teachers aren't very nice."

"And how was school for *you*?" Mom repeated.

Sasha squinted at her mom's expression. If Sasha said she hated school, could she stay at the Cirque instead?

Sasha sighed. "I like the book I'm reading." Mom's expression didn't change. "And I have lots of friends." Sasha tacked on the lie, hoping it would make Mom's eyes soften. It worked. Mom smiled.

They trekked across the Cirque grounds to the rows of cottages hidden behind a stand of tall, ancient pines.

A sharp island wind rattled through the branches, dropping needles over her mother's wild strawberry patch. The sky was a stern gray, with swathes of silver swirling through. The air smelled acidic.

"I know it's taking a little while for you to settle in," Mom said. "But your teacher says you do excellent work."

"You talk to her?"

"Of course. I want to keep up on my girl's progress."

Sasha grunted. If that was true, how come Mom didn't know how the other kids treated her? How come she ignored Sasha when she asked to stay at the Cirque instead of going to school?

Mom couldn't care *that* much.

Sasha folded her arms across her chest and glared at the ground. At Sasha's feet a bit of blue mist teased her ankles. She squinted. Mist, combined with something else. Something laced with a sinister charcoal color. Sasha's heart gave one great thump, and she held her breath. Was that . . . Smoke? Mom walked on, not noticing the Smoke, but Sasha panicked, and kicked at the air around her feet before anyone else saw the strange gray color, not stopping until the Smoke blended with the fog enough to no longer be noticeable.

Where did the Smoke come from, and why? How could it appear so close to the Light? Sasha opened her mouth to call out to her mom, but closed it abruptly and narrowed her eyes. Mom was walking through the cottage door, humming music for the new show under her breath, leaving Sasha behind. All anyone at the Cirque cared about was the new show. They didn't care that school was terrible and friends were hard to come by and that the Smoke had crept out of the shadowy forest corners where it usually lingered . . . waiting . . . watching . . . and now teased Sasha right in front of her own home.

Part of Sasha wanted to alert her mom so that the Smoke would be chased away by the power of the Light. The other part of her . . .

She wasn't exactly sure what the other part of her wanted. But she almost *liked* the Smoke. It matched her mood: sullen and stormy. She knew it couldn't stay. But here it was, teasing and taunting her, almost touching the tips of her shoes. She didn't want anyone else to know about it. She stamped her feet until the Smoke disappeared again, then let the chill of the wind fill her nostrils and ran to catch up with her mom.

"We're going to have a storm," Sasha said, shutting the cottage door behind her. She loved the rain. The heavy wetness of it, the rumbling thunder of the sky meeting earth, the white-tipped churning of the waves against the pebble shore just over the dunes ahead. "People might not come this weekend."

"It's storm season," Mom said, pulling Sasha close to her side. "There will be lots in the coming days. But we'll keep the storms at bay. We always do."

"What if one time . . . we don't?" Sasha asked.

Mom squeezed Sasha's shoulder. "It's my job to make sure we do."

Sasha nodded. The thrill of seeing Smoke for the first time faded, to be replaced by fear and uncertainty. Maybe it hadn't been Smoke at all. Maybe someone was burning leaves on the other side of the island and the dark char had traveled to the Cirque on the back of the fog. Sasha snuck her hand into her mom's and hoped she was wrong about what she'd seen.

CHAPTER 6

Sasha's mom couldn't blend into shadows like Dad could. Her feathers were every color of the rainbow, and her smile was the sun. On Friday morning before school Sasha picked her way across the muddy, rain-drenched field that led to the silver tent, so that she could watch her mom sweep across the sky with her glittering pink wings spread. Mom didn't care as much about being able to flip her hollow bones three times like Dad. Instead she tied herself around and around a big gold ribbon and stretched her flamingo legs in opposite directions.

"The audience will like the new moves yer Mom's been working on. And yer Dad. Hard workers, the both of them." Mr. Ticklefar caught up with Sasha. "It's a thing they passed along to their little girl. How's the trapeze trick coming along?"

"Fine."

Sasha squinted through the doorway of the tent. Just inside, the triplets, three contortionist sisters from the land beyond the Yellow River, arched their backs into bridges, each body stacked one on top of another, their pointed toes stretching long. Sasha always marveled at how the triplets' bones and muscles could be shaped at will. She had asked them to teach her once, when she was five and the triplets had just arrived at the Cirque, bringing with them shimmering gold bodysuits and shy smiles. They'd tried to mold Sasha's arms and legs like their own, but Sasha's limbs hadn't wanted to obey, and she'd collapsed in a heap of giggles. They'd decided contortionism wasn't for her. But she still loved to watch them practice and perform.

At least she used to. Today Sasha was impatient with everything that had to do with Cirque Magnifique. It was a feeling that had been growing in intensity since school had started. Something little, but troubling. It confused Sasha.

Yesterday at school when Toddy had come into Sasha's classroom, Jenny Myers had tried to pass him a note before Mrs. Flint took him away. But the teacher had spotted the paper, snatched it, and tossed it into the garbage. At the end of the day, Sasha had retrieved the note. When she'd uncrumpled it, she'd seen that Jenny had drawn a smiley face. How come Jenny was nice to Toddy but never tried to be nice to her? Sasha would be a good friend, if given the chance.

Sasha picked at the seam of her pants and peeked at her shoes. There it was again, that tiny waft of Smoke rising from the ground beneath her. She held back a shiver and nudged at the silvery tendrils so that Mr. Ticklefar wouldn't see it.

Once, a year ago, Sasha had slipped into Mr. Ticklefar's tent. His book of lore always seemed to be calling to her. So she had opened it and read page upon page of wonderful and terrible lore. In the very back of the book was a drawing of the Magician. He was tall and had cheeks and a chin that jutted out. His eyes, even in that sketch, had seen right through Sasha. She'd shuddered before slamming the book closed and skittering out of the tent, promising herself she would never look again.

When Sasha stared at the Smoke, it gave her that same feeling, like it could see right through her skin and into her heart. She stomped it into the ground.

Mr. Ticklefar spoke again. "Aunt Chanteuse tells me yer helping her with a new costume. Green and gold."

"It's what she wants. I'm just doing what I'm told."

"Ah." Mr. Ticklefar played with the brim of his hat.

"Hm. I thought you liked working on costumes."

Sasha did. There was delight in the feeling of silk through her fingers and joy in piecing together intricate designs, until what used to be a messy pile of tiny beads blossomed into a beautiful peony. But, like watching the triplets, creating costumes had become more tedious than fun.

Sasha looked at the triplets again. Their dark hair was cropped short so that their wide smiles were the first thing you saw when you looked at them. They were always smiling. Sasha couldn't understand it. She knew they came from a sad place. Their parents had died in terrible poverty when the triplets had been children, before they'd come to the Cirque. And yet, they loved life. Sasha wished she could be like them. But all she could do was think about what was waiting for her at school, and with those dark thoughts, the Smoke appeared at her feet again.

"I like costuming," she said quickly to Mr. Ticklefar, wishing he would move away from her.

It worked. The ringmaster slipped out of the tent before he could see the Smoke.

Sasha should have been afraid of the Smoke. She knew the things the Smoke was capable of. She even recognized the way her own heart sped up, thrumming painfully against her chest while she stood there, doing nothing. But she let the gray, sneaking tendrils work around her shoes for a little bit while Mom finished her practice. There was something thrilling about the Smoke. It was dangerous.

After Mom slid down to the ground like the flutter of a dandelion seed, she came over to Sasha and helped hoist the backpack up her shoulders. The Smoke vanished under the Light of Mom's happiness.

"This bag is too heavy. Always full of books. Where's Toddy?" Mom said. Sasha hitched her thumb over her shoulder. "You two should get going so you don't miss your bus."

"I want to stay home from school today," Sasha said, same as she did every morning.

"No, not today," Mom said, same as she did every morning. "You need a place to get away from all these adults and have a little fun with kids your own age." Sasha sighed, and Mom gathered her into a hug. Her face pressed into Mom's neck, and it smelled like the fairy floss Madame Mermadia swirled at the entrance of the big tent on Cirque nights. "I know you're having a hard time, my Sasha. Let's have friends over tonight after dinner, okay?"

Friends. Mr. Ticklefar. Aunt Chanteuse. The triplets. Were they really her friends, or were they her parents' friends?

"Fine." Sasha snapped. She let go of Mom, refusing to wave over her shoulder as she exited the silver tent.

Toddy was following the slow progress of a worm just outside the door. Mr. Ticklefar, who was a few inches shorter than Sasha even though he was years and years and years older, chatted to Toddy about worms.

". . . and the ones I saw when I was sailing down the Amazon were longer than both your arms put together."

"Have you been everywhere in the world?" Sasha said. *"Really?"*

Mr. Ticklefar squinted his one good eye, the other being hidden behind a patch—no doubt a victim of some great, horrible creature of the world—and scratched his scraggly black beard.

"I s'pose I have been everywhere, chickie. The coldest mountain tip tops to the most sweltering, inhospitable deserts. I've seen animals that looked like they were put together the wrong way and ladies covered in jewels and men wearing nothing but . . . uh, well, I should probably save that story for another day. You two better run along or you'll be missing your bus."

Sasha grasped Toddy's hand and helped him to his feet. She brushed the mud off his knees and his bangs out of his face, but Toddy shook his head defiantly until his hair was messy again. Sasha sighed. Then she laughed when Toddy looked up at her with a playful glint in his eyes.

"Come on," Sasha said, pressing her lips together and steeling herself as though she were preparing for battle.

CHAPTER 7

Sasha couldn't remember too much about the world before Toddy came into her life. She was only three when he was born, and memories didn't often stay with her at any age, slipping away like misty breath on a frost-bitten night, but she did remember the moment when she found out she had a little brother.

It was just after dawn. A flurry of early-morning activity buzzed with even more excitement than usual. The moment the big top's flag began fluttering in the warm island summer breeze, Madame Mermadia, still in her blue-and-green scale-tail costume, pushed aside the door to the tent where Sasha's mother was giving birth and looked to Sasha, who sat waiting with her dad.

But it wasn't Madame Mermadia twisting her wrists

in excitement that clued Sasha in to her new little sibling. It was the way the breeze changed directions, taking on a pleasing coolness and the scent of sweet, ripe fruit. It was the way Sasha's whole body felt lighter and the way laughter seemed to drift more effortlessly from the workhands raising the Cirque tents.

When Madame Mermadia gave them a glittering smile and a wave from the doorway, Sasha and her dad rushed into the tent. Sasha's mother lay back, exhausted, while the newborn baby gurgled, swaddled in a green-and-white-striped blanket. When Aunt Chanteuse, acting as midwife, held the baby out, Sasha's mom nestled the bundle against her chest and cooed lovingly.

Sasha waited impatiently while the baby nuzzled and nursed for the first time. Then: "Would you like to hold him, Sasha?"

She held out her arms and took him eagerly, hardly listening to the instructions that Aunt Chanteuse—who wasn't Sasha's aunt in the strictest sense, which is to say that no one knew if Aunt Chanteuse even had any brothers or sisters, but who was aunt in the Cirque sense, which is to say that *everyone* was family—rattled off to her. Sasha had been waiting for this moment for ages, at least.

"Hold one arm under his head," the elderly singer said. "Like so."

Sasha flashed a sparsely toothed three-year-old grin while their dad looked over her shoulder. The bundle was so light. Surely he would break.

"He looks just like you, 'cept you weren't so bald when you were born," Dad said. He was wearing jeans and a T-shirt, not the leotard he wore during performances, but he still moved with musical grace. "What should we call him?"

"Sasha?" she said with her soft lisp.

Dad laughed, and when he laughed, the skin at the corners of his eyes folded into dozens of trembling, paper airplane lines like the ones he folded for Sasha before shows. He kissed Sasha on top of her head and kissed the baby on top of his head too. "Let's call him Tod, after your grandfather, all right?"

"Tod is a good name," Aunt Chanteuse said. "I remember your daddy's daddy before he moved on from the Cirque. He was strong and kind, and his big arms would make you fear he could do something terrible, but he was as gentle as reeds in the breeze. He always said to me, he said, 'Aunt Chanteuse, you tell us you came from a place of bog and blight, so how come you ended up with such a pretty voice?' And I always said to him, I said, 'Tod, it's not about where we come from, but where we're going that matters.' And then he'd laugh and tip his hat at me. When he left, he became a bear, and I can just imagine him combing through downs of huckleberries on a faraway hill somewhere, softly as you please."

Sasha liked hearing stories about her grandfather. Her new brother seemed to too. The baby watched his sister with wide eyes that didn't blink. Sasha wanted to shift in the rocking chair, but she didn't dare move except to nod. "I think Tod . . . Toddy . . . Toddy is better."

"You call him Toddy, then."

Sasha beamed and caught the baby's unflinching gaze again.

In Toddy's staring eyes, tiny silver sparkles appeared, darting across the deep darkness of his irises like stars shooting across a universe. This baby, unlike other babies, was magical. She had never seen eyes like his before; she wasn't entirely sure those twinkles were possible. But she had lived a very little while and had noticed that features of many types were possible in the world. More important, she knew all things were possible through the beauty and strangeness of magic.

So Sasha held close to her brother. His joy lifted her when nothing else could tease a smile. His presence comforted her when she felt too weak to face the Islanders. One soft word could turn her frown into a smile. There was nothing she wouldn't do for him.

CHAPTER 8

On a gloomy late autumn day, Toddy came sprinting into Sasha's classroom. The new classroom assistant, Miss Islip, was right behind him, poking her head in with an apologetic smile at Ms. Terrywater.

"Come on in. The boy's right there." Ms. Terrywater pointed toward Sasha's desk before turning back to the blackboard.

"Thank you," Miss Islip whispered. Ms. Terrywater ignored her.

Miss Islip tiptoed further into the room and squatted down next to Toddy's chair. "Hey, Tod," she said. "Want to come back to class with me?"

Toddy didn't look at the teacher but kept on coloring the tulip fairy that Sasha had drawn that morning.

"He told me the other day that he likes it here," Sasha said. "He doesn't think he's learning enough in your class."

"Oh," Miss Islip said. "I didn't know he felt that way. He must be very smart."

"Toddy's very smart." Sasha frowned. "Where's Mrs. Flint?"

"Mrs. Flint will be gone for a few weeks. She tripped over one of her cats and fell down her porch steps and broke her hip. She's having a hard time getting around right now. I'm going to help Toddy in his class while Mrs. Flint is gone."

"Oh," Sasha said. Then she sat quietly while Miss Islip glanced anxiously at Ms. Terrywater, who was turned back to the class now and shooting looks full of irritated sparks their way.

"Toddy and I should get back to class. Maybe I can do the same math with him that you're doing here? Or we could color."

"Do you have fairies and pixies and tiny dragons and pirates to color?"

"I'm sure I can find something."

Sasha squeezed Toddy's hand. "Toddy will go with you, but he'd like a walk in the courtyard first."

"We can do that." Miss Islip moved closer and lowered her voice even more. "Sasha, does Toddy talk very often? He hasn't spoken to me. But the reason I'm here is to help him overcome anything that might be keeping him from talking."

"Toddy talks all the time."

"Liar," hissed a voice from the desk behind Sasha's. Kirk Stoddard leaned forward. "She's lying. That kid never talks. Ever. To anyone. He's retarded. But Sausage thinks she's a magician or something. She thinks he talks to her. All the Cirque kids are stupid, so don't believe nothing any of them says."

Sasha flinched when Kirk called her a magician. Miss Islip gazed at Kirk Stoddard steadily with those deep-lake eyes until Kirk's face turned pink and he scrunched back in his seat. Then she looked at Sasha with a different look, something softer and not just a little curious.

"I believe he talks to you," she said, and the way she said it created a flutter of hope in Sasha's belly. "Communication takes trust, and it sounds like you're a good person to trust. But he still needs to go to his own classroom."

Toddy rose from his seat, quietly returned the chair to its place against the wall, and took Miss Islip's arm. Once they'd gone and Ms. Terrywater had turned back to the blackboard to write out another problem, Kirk Stoddard leaned forward and flicked Sasha on the back of the head with his pencil.

“Ow!” Sasha rubbed the sore spot.

“You think that’s bad, Sausage Brown? Wait and see what I’ve got planned for you after school.”

At the end of the school day, Sasha packed her things under the watchful eye of her teacher, Ms. Terrywater, then went to the other side of the school building to pick up Toddy. Her stomach had ached ever since Kirk Stoddard had talked to her, but seeing Toddy made her feel better.

In the days before Mrs. Flint fell over her cat, Toddy would sit in a chair facing the narrow, dirty windows that looked out onto the courtyard. His teacher sat at her desk, face buried in a book or filing her nails. Mrs. Flint would ignore Sasha as she walked in and stood next to Toddy, looking out over the weed-filled courtyard with him. She spoke only when she got tired of looking at the two motionless, scrawny backs.

“Go home,” Mrs. Flint would mutter as she shaped her pinkie nail to a sharp tip.

The brand-new assistant teacher, Miss Islip, would poke her head up, a guilty expression softening the timid lines of her face. Sasha had always suspected that Miss Islip was very nice, but the teacher was too intimidated to ask Mrs. Flint to not speak so cruelly to the children. But today the room seemed bigger and more airy. There was a sweet, lemony smell drifting by, and giggles from the corner by the window.

"Sasha," Miss Islip said, waving her over. "I was just pointing out the pixies to your brother."

Sasha ran to join them. "We do that all the time too. But Mrs. Flint always says there's nothing out there and to stop being ridiculous and to *go home.*"

Miss Islip's eyes were sad, two emeralds that had lost their shine. She played with the long silver chain around her neck. At the bottom was a cone-shaped rainbow pendant. "I know. I'm sorry she always said that. Since she's not here, we can look until we get tired of looking. Until our eyeballs fall out!"

Sasha shivered and giggled at the same time. It would be so horribly funny for their eyeballs to fall out and roll around on the floor. But there wasn't time to see if that was even possible. "We have to catch the bus home."

"Oh, of course."

As they left the classroom, Sasha glanced over her shoulder. Miss Islip seemed different. It was as though she could see Toddy's magic, now that Mrs. Flint wasn't around to cast a shadow over it. Sasha wished she could change everyone on that side of the island. She thought it was awful that they didn't have a Light in their lives.

CHAPTER 9

The moldering train tracks that crossed the island from the old docks to the center of town, at one point cresting the hill between the Cirque and the town, were a popular place to play after school. Stray animals made homes in burrows dug under the unused railroad ties. The tall meadows were perfect for organizing a game of tag or searching for anthills to investigate.

The sky was the rich blue of Madame Mermadia's sea princess costume. The sun lingered like it didn't want to release autumn and give winter the reins. A dozen schoolmates, at least, took advantage of the weather, playing at the tracks.

When the school bus pulled away that December

afternoon, Sasha and Toddy stood, hand in hand, watching everyone play.

I have lots of friends.

That's what Sasha had told her mom. It had been a lie, the only one she could ever remember telling her mom. And it poked at her painfully, like when she pricked her finger with a sewing needle.

She needed to make it a truth. There were so many things about her that would make her a good friend: stories of weird and wonderful creatures, tumbling skills she could teach to everyone, staunch loyalty.

"Come on," she said to Toddy.

The brother and sister walked toward their schoolmates instead of the Cirque. The girls sat, dotted like a flock of birds on a patch of grass, picking wildflowers to weave into bracelets or crowns. Sasha searched for Jenny, but the flaxen-haired girl wasn't there. The boys gathered in a circle next to the tracks, some standing and some squatting, with their attention focused on an object in the middle.

They all ignored Sasha and Toddy walking ever closer. But Toddy's curiosity got the better of him, and he pulled his hand free from Sasha's, skipping over to the tracks.

"Come back!" Sasha kept her voice low so the boys wouldn't hear her. But the boys didn't look at her; they were too busy with whatever was in the circle. Some of the girls looked up and, even though Sasha gave them her most glowing smile in the hopes they would invite her over to play, they sneered and looked away.

Toddy elbowed his way through the crowd. He was so much smaller than the rest of them that they hardly noticed he was there.

In the center of the circle, one eye dripping blood-tinged tears, was a fluffy gray-striped kitten. It eyed the boys warily with its one good eye, its body pulled back into itself and its fur standing on end. It mewed pathetically.

The boys laughed and yelled, each one shouting louder than the one before him, trying to gain Kirk Stoddard's attention.

"Wonder where its mommy is."

"Kirk, you're an amazing shot. Nailed the little piss right in the eye from twenty yards away."

"I know."

"I'll hold it still if you want to try to get the other eye," said Colton Markson.

Toddy gasped and flung himself wildly into the middle of the circle, falling on his hands and knees over the kitten, shrieking, "No!" At his yell, Sasha pushed and shoved, desperately trying to get past the outer ring of the circle and to her brother.

"What the hell?" Colton said. "Isn't that the stupid Brown kid? What's he doing here?"

The boys in the circle followed Colton's lead, throwing out cusses and exclamations. Scott Maillard lifted his foot and balanced it on Toddy's side, and then pushed him over into the dirt. The kitten took the opportunity to dash under Scott's leg and away from the group. Its gray-and-white tail was last seen darting under a railroad tie.

Kirk Stoddard entered the circle and stood next to Toddy. "Now look what you did, you little piss. You let our cat get away." He squatted down and lifted Toddy's chin so that he could stare into Toddy's face. Toddy looked to the right, the left, anywhere but into Kirk's blazing eyes. "You wanna be our toy instead? Huh? Why don't you look at me, you little freak? Those creepy eyes . . ." Kirk gave an exaggerated shudder, the boys behind him breaking into peals of laughter. "If you don't look, you won't be able to duck when my fist comes flying."

"Leave him alone," Sasha screamed. She elbowed Colton as hard as she could, causing him to double over with a groan, and entered the circle to stand over her brother. They might threaten her, but she would protect Toddy. "Stop it! He didn't do anything to you."

Kirk stood up again, taller than anyone else there. "Sausage Brown," he spit. "You want to fight me? Nah,

I don't fight girls. Especially ones that stink like you. They're weak. Ain't no fun."

"But you'll fight little boys half your size? Oh, how strong you are." Sasha jammed her fists into her hips.

Kirk took a step back, shocked, but only for a second. His mouth and eyes twisted with rage, and he pushed back again, stepping farther and farther from the brother and sister crouching in the middle of the spectators, his hands clenched into fists around the jagged rocks he carried.

"Want me to hold 'em?" Scott asked with a smirk.

"Nah, it'll be more sporting to let them run. I can still hit 'em."

Sasha and Toddy didn't move, frozen in place by confusion.

"You'd better run," Colton mocked. "Unless you like getting beat on."

The circle of boys widened as they broke formation. Two boys gathered their own rocks from the banks of the railroad tracks. Others watched as Kirk lined himself up and squinted his eyes, aiming for his target. He raised his arm and let the first rock fly. It shot through the air like a bullet and glanced off the tip of Toddy's ear.

The boys' laughter broke the tense silence like the roar of an ocean wave. Toddy raised his hand to his ear in surprise.

"You better run," Colton said again, through his giggles.

Sasha pushed Toddy behind her, protecting him with her slim body. Kirk moved closer to join his friends again, raised his arm, and launched another rock. It hit Sasha square in the chest with a thud. She gasped. The laughter rang louder. Some of the girls stopped playing with the flowers and approached the scene and picked up their own rocks.

An uncontrollable thickness, like simmering lava in the depths of a volcano, welled up in Sasha's stomach. The spot where the rock had hit her didn't hurt, but her belly did. She faltered under the heavy pressure on her lungs, the pushing of air against her chest so hard that she couldn't take any air in herself. She gagged, sucking down oxygen with a stuttered *gahk-a-rattle-rattle.* Sasha clutched Toddy's fingers fiercely and glared at the boys. Their hands were held high, their palms full of pebbles and gravel. Their faces were blurry.

"Sasha?" From beside her came the whispered voice, shaky, catching on the *sh* in the middle of her name.

"Let's go," Sasha said.

She took a first hesitant step backward, keeping her eyes on the boys and their creeping smiles. They didn't move any closer, but their arms didn't drop down either. She stepped back again, moving Toddy with her.

When Kirk Stoddard, leading the charge up front, laughed and threw his arm forward again, Sasha and Toddy turned and fled. A shower of stones fell upon their backs and tangled in their hair as they ran along the train tracks. The laughter of the girls leaped up and down their arms like tiny, clawing bugs.

The island kids didn't give chase, but terror sped Sasha and Toddy on. Neither looked back as they ran up the railroad tracks. Their attention was completely taken by the railroad ties. They stepped carefully so that they wouldn't trip on the wood.

The volcano simmering in Sasha's chest began to blow, the lava making its way up her esophagus, burning the places below her collarbones. One last far-flung rock hit Toddy on the head and set the volcano to erupting. Tears poured from Sasha's eyes, disrupting her sight so that the railroad ties and gravel were nothing more than swimming colors of brown, then black, then brown again. Everything tinged with flame-orange.

When the toe of her shoe caught under a tie, at a place where the gravel had been worn away by wind and time and digging feet, Sasha went flying into a patch of sharp-edged rocks, and Toddy went down with her.

Sasha stayed on the ground. She breathed in the dirt until her heart slowed. A sharp pain pricked one side of her face. She wished for home, for a quiet moment with paper and pencils, sketching things delightful, or for the raucous joy of Cirque friends and storytelling filling every corner of the cottage.

"Toddy?" She turned her head to the side to see where he'd fallen. He hunched over his legs a couple of feet away, holding his knee in his hands. "Are you hurt?"

Sasha pushed herself up, ignoring the scrapes on her palms, and crawled to her little brother. He looked at her with watery eyes and brushed his sleeve under his nose. "I'm okay."

Sasha moved his hand aside. She gazed at his knee, dark pink and roughed-up skin but no blood, and sighed. "I'm sorry. I didn't mean to make them mad. It's my fault they hurt you."

"You didn't make them throw the rocks." Toddy shook his head and pointed to her cheek. "You have a rock in your face."

Sasha drew her eyebrows together and touched her cheek tentatively. Just under her eye, at the spot where her cheekbones jutted out, was a small, tender bump. She winced as she rubbed her finger across the skin. Then she looked back the way they had come. "We should go home so Mom can get this out. And so we can clean your knee."

Toddy pushed himself off the ground and held out his hand to his sister. They stood, neither of them wanting to go back the way they'd come. "Do you think they're still there?"

Sasha shrugged. Would the boys hang around to see if she and Toddy returned? Wouldn't they have better things to do than wait for them to come back to the crossroads? What if they didn't and were expecting Sasha and Toddy to come running home like scaredy-cats?

The sister and brother sat on the side of the train tracks until the sun was nearly level with the top of the hill.

"We'd better go home," Sasha said. She took Toddy's hand. "Hopefully they've gone by now."

They crept down, but when they reached the spot where the other kids had run them off, it was silent and empty.

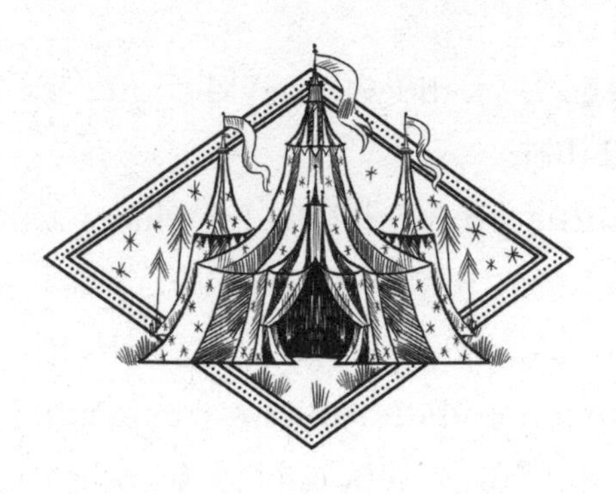

CHAPTER 10

Cirque Magnifique performed on Friday, Saturday, and Sunday. Sasha and Toddy liked to sit near the old train tracks and watch for the first set of lights at the top of the hill that told them the ferry had arrived and the audience was on its way. The lights came, breaking the indigo twilight with beams of yellow, and came some more as the cars descended into the valley, a single line of people mesmerized with the possibility that they, too, would touch a bit of magic that night.

Cirque Magnifique's shows were always sold out, the big tent always full of travelers from just across the sound, from over vast seas, from beyond mountains and deserts. They were tourists from all the far-flung locations of Sasha's imagination. The only people who never came to the shows were the people who lived on the other side of the island. They avoided the Cirque at all costs.

Sasha sighed when the last car topped the hill and began descending down to the Cirque. She stood slowly, her body aching all over, and took her brother's hand.

"Come on. Storm's going to be back on tonight."

The storm season had kept its promise, as it did every year, bringing magnificent squalls to the island, but tonight the drops held off until every last ticket holder was safe and warm inside the big tent, and then the skies opened, pouring buckets of rain, joining the audience's applause until it sounded like the whole world was being trampled under the thundering of horses.

Sasha paced in the dressing tent, pulling her hair tightly back from her face and yanking on the straps of her leotard. The costume was getting too small—or she was getting too big—and the straps dug into her shoulders. Mom noticed and promised a new one before tomorrow night's show.

"You're going to be amazing tonight," Mom said.

It was the first night of the new show, *Reflections*, and the first time Sasha and Dad would perform their new trick. But Sasha was disgruntled. Her parents didn't know just how not-amazing she was. Which was why Sasha hid all the school event notices and pretended school conferences never happened. Her mom said she kept up on Sasha's progress in school, but Sasha never asked what her mom and her teacher talked about. She didn't want the shame of her family knowing how awful she was.

Sasha sighed. Her fingers twitched around the book she'd brought into the dressing tent—it was such a luscious fantasy—but even that story had lost its luster. With a frown, Sasha pitched the book under her mom's makeup table to gather dust, then plopped on the floor, joining Toddy and the puzzle he was putting together until it was her turn to make an appearance in the big tent.

Toddy was the only one in the family who didn't have a part in the show. Tonight Sasha wished she didn't have a part either. She wanted to sit on the floor and listen to the rain and curl under a blanket with her brother when the inevitable thunder began its rumble across the sky.

Aunt Chanteuse was putting her makeup on in front of the big mirror and caught Sasha's eye in the reflection. The old woman pursed her red lips, seeming to know what dark thoughts permeated Sasha's mind, so Sasha looked away quickly. She was tired of having to pretend everything was all right. Instead, she watched her mom choose a glittering headdress for her performance.

"Jenny Myers is having a slumber party tonight and she invited all the girls from our class," Sasha said to her mom, as she tugged at the leotard straps again. Sasha didn't know why she told her mom about the party. She never told her mom about the things that happened at school.

Mom paused with a red feathered headdress in her hands. "Why didn't you bring me the invitation? We would have let you go. I'm sure one of the stagehands could have taken you over in their truck after the trapeze."

"Because she invited everyone but me."

"Why would she do that?"

It was the first time Mom had asked Sasha that question—why?—and she looked genuinely puzzled. Mom thought Sasha was a different person than everyone else thought she was, Sasha figured. Mom didn't know the truth, that Sasha was horrible. Unlikeable. A freak. Sasha knew things about Smoke and Light that the other kids didn't know, and they mocked her for knowing. They all hated her, and it was Cirque Magnifique's fault. It was her mom's fault, for coming to the Cirque in the first place. It was her dad's fault for being here even before that. And it was both their faults for not knowing how she and Toddy were treated. It all made Sasha furious.

She threw a puzzle piece onto the floor and pushed

her fists into her eyes. The air in the room changed, becoming heavier and taking on a slightly sour smell. "Because we're the Cirque freaks! Everyone hates us."

"Sasha. That's not true."

"Yes, it is! They make fun of Toddy and call us names and won't play with us at recess." Sasha opened her eyes and stared at her mom. But something else caught her attention. Smoke lingered lazily at the edges of the dressing tent entrance, as though waiting for an invitation to come all the way in. The color on the bottom of the walls began to fade, and a pinch of dust fluttered down from the ceiling. "I wish I were a normal island kid and not a Cirque freak. I wish I had a pretty house like Leslie and normal clothes like—"

"What's wrong with your clothes? I can take you shopping tomorrow morning, if you want."

Sasha huffed. She felt like she was growing. Being filled with something hazy and thick. "I don't just want new clothes. I don't want to be here at all. I don't want all these other freaks around us. I want . . . a new life. I want a new family. One that's normal. I hate this. And I hate all of you!"

Sasha's mom picked up the puzzle piece Sasha had thrown and gently set it on the floor near Toddy. She stood. The beads on her costume rattled and glinted. Normally Sasha would think the rows of glitter the most beautiful thing in the world, like jeweled lamps bobbing on dusky water, but right now it all looked garish. The colors gleamed at her maliciously, taunting her with their brilliance.

Mom brought Sasha's fists to her daughter's side slowly and brushed the hair out of her face. "Every family who loves as much as we do is normal, even if we seem different from every other person in the world." She tucked a finger under Sasha's leotard strap and frowned. "You're right. This is much too small. Why don't you take the night off? I'll do your part, and you can finish the puzzle with your brother. Tomorrow we'll go to the store."

"I don't want to take the night off, and I don't want to go to the store. I want to . . ." And finally Sasha yelled the thing she wanted most, the terrifying and awful thing she wanted to happen to the Cirque. "I want to disappear. I want us all to disappear forever!"

Aunt Chanteuse chirped disapprovingly. "Miss Sasha! That is not a thing you wish on your worst enemy."

"I don't want to wish it on them. I want to wish it on me! I want the Smoke to come and gulp us down!"

"Oh!" Aunt Chanteuse gave a last sweep of her makeup brush and stood.

Sasha's mom said nothing more, but she gathered

her daughter in her arms and held her tightly, then let go and left for the big tent with Aunt Chanteuse. The mix of anger and sadness rolling in Sasha's chest confused her. She wanted to do her job, because she loved responsibility, but she didn't want to do it, because it made her a freak.

"I don't want the Smoke to come," Toddy said calmly. He didn't look up at Sasha—she wasn't sure she could handle the look in his eyes if he *did*—but Sasha could feel waves of disappointment rolling off him.

I don't want it to come for you, Sasha wanted to say, but her tongue seemed to twist in ten different directions and she couldn't get the words out.

Instead Sasha plopped onto the floor and immersed herself in the puzzle so that the icky feeling in her chest would go away. She thought if she ignored it long enough, it would fade, but many minutes later, with the moon overhead and surges of lightning cutting the sky, Sasha still had the urge to scream and cry. The feeling had only gotten worse. A simmering, dark thing. The puzzle was finished by now, and Toddy was curled up with a book. Sasha couldn't sit still, though. Smoke kept filtering into the tent, and Sasha watched it obsessively. Would it be better if they all transformed now and went into the world in their new animal disguises? What did it mean for it to be someone's time, anyway? No one had ever told her the whole story of what the Magician had done all those years ago, but she wanted to know. She wanted it to happen again. Sasha was so tired of the way people treated her that she was *sure* it was her time. Time to run away, time for relief from the things that squeezed her heart until it felt as shriveled and tiny as a raisin.

Sasha looked at her brother. He looked content, and that made Sasha even angrier. How could he be so calm?

"I'm going to the big tent," Sasha announced. She had to get away from all the quiet in the dressing tent. It helped her think too much. "Stay out of trouble," she said to her brother. Toddy didn't answer, but he turned the page in his book and kept reading, and Sasha thought that was as good as a yes.

Sasha pulled her ballet flats on, snapping the elastic across the top of her foot so that it smarted, smoothed her flyaway hairs as best she could back into her snug ponytail, and ducked into the rainy night.

CHAPTER 11

There was a secret flap in the back of the big tent that led to the shadows under the bleachers. Sasha ducked under the fabric and made her way through a tunnel of audience members, who clapped and shouted for the tricks they were watching, and skirted the area where Mr. Ticklefar raised and lowered, raised and lowered the music so that swells of trumpets and rolls of drums trembled in every body in the tent. The thunder outside was louder, though. Sasha felt the electricity of the lightning as her hairs stood at attention on her arms. There was something wrong about tonight, and she didn't know if it had caused her to say those terrible things to her mom, or if the wrongness had all started when she'd said them.

Dad was already performing, twisting his dark body through the air as the lights flickered every color in the rainbow. Aunt Chanteuse was on the floor, in front of where the net used to be, her green-and-gold dress shimmering under the lights, her voice soaring above all the other noise. Mom stood where Sasha should be, waiting for the right moment to send the bar across the air for Dad to catch.

The new flip was coming up soon; Sasha would have to fly up the ladder to get there in time to take Mom's place and do the job herself. Her head told her to stay where she was; her body, though, moved automatically, drawn to the platform. She sprinted, pumping her arms and legs across the back of the stage. With the lights directed above, the ground was as black as a starless night, and Sasha collided with the corner of a box, slamming her shin into the wood.

"Oww!" she hollered. With the music so loud, no one could hear her, but she clapped one hand over her mouth anyway and squeezed her eyes shut until the first waves of sharp pain subsided.

That horrible smell surrounded her again. She knew the Smoke was swirling near, even though she couldn't see it. Part of her was glad—the part that didn't want to go up the ladder. The rest of her made her body get up again, reach for the ladder, and clamber over each rung.

She wasn't going to make it.

Aunt Chanteuse's voice nearly lifted the roof off the big tent. Mom squeezed her knuckles around the bar, her eyes focused on Dad, flinging himself nearly to the tip-top of the big tent. He twisted, flipped. The audience gasped. Sasha's foot slipped off the rung, shaking the pillar. Mom looked down. Their eyes caught, and the deepest sadness Sasha had ever seen filled her mom's face. Then Mom let go of the bar.

A second too late.

"No! No!" Sasha screamed.

The audience screamed with joyful anticipation. Mom looked in horror, frozen to her spot with her arms still high. Dad flipped again and raised his arms out for the bar that was supposed to meet him, his bright grin confident and sure. But there was only air.

Smoke rose quickly from under the tent, obscuring the ground. It brought a low, menacing laughter with it. Sasha's eyes watered, and her nose began to run. Aunt Chanteuse's voice cut off abruptly. And there were Dad's hands, palms open, waiting, expecting, counting on Sasha to have done her job correctly. There was nothing to meet him.

The audience's yells of delight changed to screams of terror as Dad fell . . . fell . . . fell all the way past where the net should have been and into the waiting arms of the Smoke billowing up from the ground. Mom reached for Dad, as though her arms were long enough to catch him, and tumbled off the platform.

"Dad!" Sasha screamed. "Mom!"

She raced back down the ladder, but the lower she got, the harder it was to see. The Smoke kept growing, blinding everyone in the big tent with its sinister darkness. Sasha stumbled left and right. She bumped into adults and children and animals, all fleeing for the exits. Aunt Chanteuse reached through the Smoke for Sasha, but Sasha pushed her away. She didn't need help.

Sasha searched and searched, tears streaming down her face as the Smoke pecked and itched at every inch of her skin. Finally Sasha saw a large, black-and-white bird battling through the Smoke, its oily feathers beating furiously for the door at the side of the big tent. The Smoke coiled around its wings and pulled the bird down, pinning the animal to the ground. The bird's fierce beak snapped and gnashed until the Smoke retreated, but only long enough for the Smoke to gather into an even larger ball of darkness and attack again.

This was what Sasha had wanted, but now that the Smoke was here, now that it was claiming people before their time, Sasha's anger and sadness twisted with a new burst of terror. She leaped in between the ball of Smoke and the bird. The Smoke pushed her down furiously, but Sasha's movement gave the bird enough time to lift itself with one last, great stretch of his wings and push from the tent and into the night sky. Within seconds a wind fluttered past Sasha's ear and a second bird, this one a flash of brilliant colors, chased the black-and-white bird into the ether. Sasha ran for the exit to catch a last glimpse of her parents soaring into the dark of the storm. She paused. Picked something up.

"Mom. Dad."

All that was left of them was a feather.

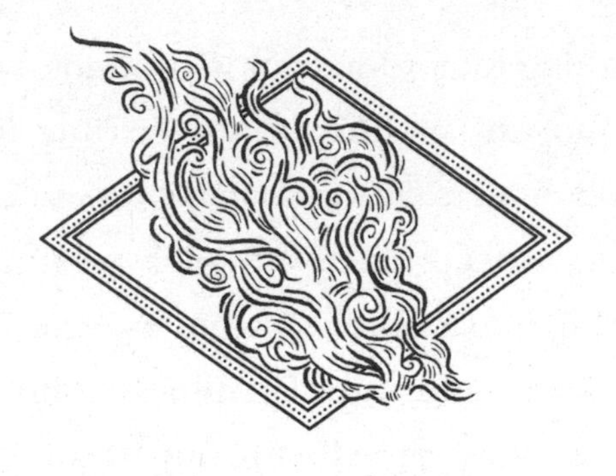

CHAPTER 12

Hail battered the line of cars as the audience rushed away from Cirque Magnifique and to the ferry that would take them far away from the island. Winds whipped the tents, ripping the glittering flags from their poles and sending them over the water in the distance. Smoke billowed and rolled until the last visitor was out of sight, and then it finally settled like a blanket over the grounds. The Cirque performers retreated to their cottages, huddling together and watching out the windows anxiously, hoping the Smoke and storm would all blow over. Hoping their Light would come back. Hoping they wouldn't all be taken before their time.

Late in the night the sky was silenced, at last. Toddy had come to join Sasha in the big tent, adding his steady, quiet breathing to her loud, snotty sounds. Sasha sat in the same spot she had for hours, twirling the feather between her fingers. It was black in the center, slowly changing to a deep amethyst color moving outward, before flaring into a vibrant magenta at the tip.

Mr. Ticklefar and Aunt Chanteuse joined the children. The big tent gaped with hugeness, having only the four of them in it. No glitter, no music, no applause. Only the fog and chill of Smoke.

"We've canceled the rest of the shows this weekend," Mr. Ticklefar growled. He twisted his mustache haphazardly, as though he didn't know what else to do with his hands. "The Smoke seems to be . . . holding back . . . for now. You two should go to bed."

"I won't sleep," Sasha said. "I can't ever sleep again. This is all my fault."

"Don't you say that, little Sasha. It weren't yer fault at all! 'Twas the Smoke. That dastardly devilish Magician that cursed us well before you or I was born."

"But I let the Smoke in. I know I did." Sasha's voice dropped to a whisper. "I said the most terrible thing. Mom thinks I hate her. She probably hates me! It's just that . . . I *do* want to disappear. I hate it here!"

"Oh, child." Aunt Chanteuse hummed.

"Impossible on all counts," Mr. Ticklefar said. "I think yer just overtired. Get some sleep. I'm sure . . . uh . . .

yer mom and dad will rush back to you first thing in the morning."

Mr. Ticklefar tried to sound sure. His face tried to look brave. But Sasha saw the way his heavy left eyebrow twitched and how he couldn't quite look her in the eye. The Smoke was tricky and devious. Mom and Dad would never be back. The thing was, she'd wanted the Smoke to take only her, not anyone else. She shook her head. It was all she could do. Her mouth, she discovered, could not open. Sasha would never speak again.

There were beans and bread for dinner because Sasha refused to go to the dining tent with the rest of the Cirque. Their frightened faces made her fingers tremble. They had done so much for her, and what had she done?

Invited the Smoke in.

She took stock of the supplies in the pantry and wondered how long she and Toddy could avoid the outside world. Her glued-together mouth kept her from eating, so she figured she and Toddy would be all right for a while, since it was only Toddy who needed to be fed.

Sasha heated the can of beans in a small pot and served half of them to Toddy. They watched each other in silence while he dipped his bread into his bowl and ate. Sasha frowned quizzically when Toddy saved a small bit of bread and beans in a jar and screwed the lid tightly. But she just shook her head and helped him wash his dishes when he was done, then put the leftovers in the fridge. Then they lay down, side by side, on their bed.

"Do you think Mom will be all right in the storm?" Toddy asked.

Sasha nodded.

"And Dad? And we'll be all right too?"

Another nod.

"Do you want to go to the shore and find sea glass?"

Sasha shook her head slowly.

"Right. Maybe when it stops raining?"

Sasha squeezed her eyes shut. Toddy put his arm around his sister and snuggled close to her. "I think you're nice," he said.

Sasha put her fingers on the side of Toddy's face and smiled at him. She closed her eyes and sighed through her nose and rolled over to sleep.

CHAPTER 13

A storm wept and howled for the next two days. Sasha got up each morning and helped Toddy cook breakfast and waited patiently for the glue on her mouth to dissolve. Her belly, thick with pain and hard to carry when their parents had left, was now hollow and light. It seemed unconnected to the rest of her body, groaning and gurgling at her angrily.

Mr. Ticklefar and Aunt Chanteuse came and knocked on the cottage door regularly, but Sasha refused to open it. So they spoke through the door, telling Sasha and Toddy that their parents would be home soon. But Sasha didn't believe them. No one came back, once they'd transformed and left the Cirque.

On the third day Sasha and Toddy prepared for

school once again. Toddy ate a breakfast of boiled rice and canned apple pie filling. He scooped two spoonfuls of leftovers into a small container. Sasha raised her eyebrows at him.

"It's for later," Toddy said.

The walk took twice as long as usual, with Sasha stopping every few feet to suck air greedily in through her nose and let it out again, and when they arrived at the bus stop, the bus was gone. They'd missed it. So they walked on. Sasha stopped once they reached town, and stared into the glistening windows of the ice cream parlor. The colors of the candies and treats swam before her, the jellies and gummies melting into monstrous, mocking shapes, and the lollipops opening wide mouths to gape at her. But she closed her eyes to the horrors and breathed in the thick scent wafting out of the mail slot in the door.

Toddy put his arm around his sister and helped move her along. Sasha smiled at her brother gratefully as they finished their walk to school.

Ms. Terrywater noticed Sasha long enough to ask if Sasha had an absence slip from the office and to sigh when Sasha shook her head silently.

"Have you been sick? You look like you still are," the teacher said. Sasha said nothing. "Sit down, then. I'll call your mother at lunch."

Sasha hesitated at the door. How could she tell Mrs.

Terrywater that her parents were gone . . . and it was all her fault? Flashes of orange and yellow light swam around the rim of her vision, and she swayed. She didn't want to sit in her usual seat, with Kirk Stoddard just behind it. He glared at her and mouthed the word *Sausage.*

It took a great deal of effort to compose her swimming head and defy Ms. Terrywater, but Sasha swallowed the dryness that made her mouth feel like sawdust and shook her head.

"Sasha Brown, sit yourself down."

Kirk laughed at the rhyme. He repeated it to Colton in a high, squeaky voice.

Sasha rubbed at the sepia smudges under her eyes and obeyed. Her seat was cool through her thin skirt, and she shivered uncontrollably as the cold met the warmth of the back of her legs.

"You look dead," Kirk hissed.

Sasha focused on keeping her drooping lids open. Ms. Terrywater was asking for volunteers to fix the grammatical errors in a sentence on the board. Every time her teacher put chalk to board, Sasha cringed.

"You shaking? Huh, dirty Sausage Brown?" Kirk leaned forward and laughed, but settled back in his seat as Ms. Terrywater's eyes swept over them. She held her hand out, the tip of the chalk pointing accusingly.

"Sasha, do you want to fix the sentence?"

Sasha could see the mistakes: the missing capitals in the name, the misspelling of "kangaroo," the question mark instead of a period. But Sasha shook her head.

"That's 'cause Sausage's as stupid as her brother," Colton said, leaning into the aisle so Sasha would hear him.

"Colton. How nice of you to volunteer. Come to the board please."

"Shoot," he muttered. He shot Sasha a murderous look as he made his way to the front of the classroom. Kirk laughed at Colton's back.

The top of Sasha's desk was covered in shapeless gouges and names written in loopy handwriting. She ran her finger over some of them, tracing the canyons and crests and wishing she could slip from her seat and dive into them. Rivers ran through canyons. She wondered if she, like her parents, could shift into an animal, and if she could, she would choose to be a fish and swim and swish through canyons all day long. Sasha tilted her head toward her desk, hoping to change right then and there.

"Hey, Sausage, stay awake. No sleeping in class. Lazy freak."

Kirk tugged on her hair. A moment later the weight of her head lightened. She spun around in her seat to see a pile of her hair in the middle of Kirk's desk. He stared back at her with drooping eyes, his fingers curled through the handles of his scissors and a clump of brown in his other fist.

She couldn't scream, but her eyes blazed passionate fury as she stood, clutching the back of her head. Kirk's mouth turned up at the corners as Sasha swayed to the side, bumping her hip into her desk and stumbling into the aisle. Her vision darkened around the edges.

Kirk dropped the hair and scissors onto his desk and folded his arms across his chest. Somewhere behind Sasha someone said her name. It was far, far away, though, and she didn't pay it much heed. Instead she snatched up Kirk's scissors and pointed them at him.

The tip of the scissors was blunt, but that didn't stop Kirk's eyes from widening. The blades were sharp. Sasha's name was called again, but her eyes flashed strobes of light and her brain screamed in torment, though hampered by the soundproof walls of her lips. She didn't blink. Her dry eyes itched.

Sasha gripped a hunk of what was left of her hair in her fist and put the scissors to it, then sawed at the strands like a frantic woodcutter. When the hunk fell away, she flung it at Kirk and reached for another. Her name came again, followed by a clapping sound. The second clump soared over Kirk's head. Hands reached for her from behind, demanding, shouting at her. But she was deaf to the words. She cut again and again, nicking her fingers, only pausing in her cutting to swat at the bees that were stinging her arms, that were trying to take her scissors away from her.

"Sasha!"

Noise grew around Sasha. Ms. Terrywater's low heels tapping toward her, Colton swearing loudly from the front of the room, and Kirk breathing hard. Kirk's eyes were huge with fear. He deserved it. He deserved to be afraid of her, like she used to be of him. He brushed her hair out of his face, off his head and his desk, with the desperation of brushing away a disease, but Sasha kept throwing the pieces at him.

Oh, she wanted to scream at him. She wanted to open her mouth and blast him with the force of her words.

She paused when the scissors blade caught her ear. The room swirled. Pressure built in her throat. She would vomit, but there was nothing to vomit and nowhere for it to go.

Sasha's name was spoken again as she fell to her knees and grasped for her desk. It wasn't where it was supposed to be. Where was she? Close to the ground, and black everywhere.

Someone spoke next to her ear. ". . . Band-Aid from the nurse. Hurry up!"

"She's crazy," the boy, that boy, whispered at her.

Sasha balled her hands into fists and rubbed at her eyes, they itched so much. The floor, murky linoleum with swirls of blue and green, was right there, just beyond her face. *A fish. Make me into one of Mr. Ticklefar's weird and wonderful fishes from the far corners of the earth, and let me swim away.* But the cold floor stayed hard and impenetrable, and her hands remained hands and her feet remained feet, and magic and Light were so far away, like they had abandoned her. Sasha pressed her cheek to the stream-like swirls on the floor and closed her eyes against the cold, moving her arms in a swimming motion, kicking her leg-fins, hoping . . . hoping.

"Kirk Stoddard, what have I told you about pulling those scissors out when you're not supposed to? One day you'll slip and hurt yourself," Ms. Terrywater scolded. Then, more gently: "Sit up, Sasha." There was a sound of tearing paper followed by a warm tug on her ear. Something was drawn through the remains of her hair. "Short hair looks pretty on a little face like yours."

Someone said the words, and it sounded like her mother's voice, though it couldn't possibly have been her mother speaking because her mother trilled now.

A pair of hands fitted under her arms and lifted her to her seat. "You weigh nothing," that voice said.

Sasha surveyed the room. Every pair of eyes looked back at her, some with curiosity, some with disgust, some with pity. Jenny Myers hovered in the aisle, fighting back tears and still holding the wrapping from the bandage. At the chalkboard Colton stood with his mouth hanging open and his hand held high. But the piece of chalk he'd been writing with had long since fallen to the floor.

Ms. Terrywater was the only person who moved, and her eyes were filled with so much sorrow for Sasha. The rest of them were as still as evergreens on a windless day. Even their breathing paused as they anticipated Sasha's next move. She moved her gaze to the glass tank near the windows and locked eyes with Scrubbles the turtle. It looked back at her as though it understood everything. *I'm trapped here too.*

Ms. Terrywater went to her desk and filled out the top page on a pad of hall passes. She marched back toward Sasha, who closed her eyes and prepared to be in trouble. But the teacher didn't stop at Sasha's desk. Ms. Terrywater held the slip out to Kirk Stoddard, who gritted his teeth when he saw what the slip said.

"To the principal, now," Ms. Terrywater said. Her voice was dark and heavy, and her eyes were glittering crystals of ice.

Kirk took the paper and stood noisily. He didn't look at Sasha, or at anyone else, as he made his way out of the classroom.

Sasha rested her cheek on her desk. When Ms. Terrywater turned back toward the front of the room, she paused next to Sasha, placed her hand on Sasha's head, and murmured, "Yes, you rest awhile."

CHAPTER 14

Sasha waited in the hallway for Toddy to slip out of his classroom and meet her for the recess time before lunch. He was too busy fastening bells to ribbons to see her, but from the doorway to Toddy's room, Miss Islip raised her hand in a wave.

Then she got a good look at Sasha. She yelped, "Sasha Brown!"

Miss Islip stretched a shaking hand to Sasha's shoulder, studying the girl's face, taking in the sunken cheeks, the eyes with circles like raccoons', the dry lips. Under Miss Islip's fingers, the shoulder was bony, the skin stretched like the latex on an overblown balloon.

"When's the last time you ate, Sasha?"

Sasha stared at Miss Islip with eyes that were too

big for her face. Two wide gray circles as flat as pocked cement.

"Ms. Terrywater," Miss Islip cried as she spotted Sasha's teacher in the hallway. "What—"

"I've tried calling home, but no one's answering. Sasha won't give me any details, but I understand there was an accident involving her parents a little while back at the Cirque. I'll try again this afternoon, but right now I have recess duty." Ms. Terrywater rushed after the rest of her class, pulling apart two boys shoving each other down the hall. Sasha sighed through her nose, and Miss Islip pursed her lips.

"Toddy, you wait here in the classroom. Sasha, come with me. Let's get you some help."

Sasha sank all her weight into her heels and shook her head. Sasha had destroyed her whole world when she'd let the Smoke in, and now she was beyond help.

Miss Islip peered into Sasha's face. "What is it? Why won't you come with me?"

Sasha raised her chin defiantly, but Miss Islip knew something about being stubborn too. The teacher took Sasha's hand firmly and marched her down the hallway. The silver-and-rainbow necklace Miss Islip always wore clinked with each step. They rounded the corner into the cafeteria, where the distinctive school smells of melted cheese and fried potatoes filled Sasha's nose.

"You know we serve breakfast here, right? And that it can be free. Breakfast, and lunch, too. Why don't your parents sign up for these things? Why does no one else think to take care of it? Your teacher? Don't they see you starv—like this?" Miss Islip rapped at the glass food service barriers and smiled impatiently when a tall man with a shiny, bald head sauntered out from the back.

"Hello, Miss Islip," he drawled. Sasha smiled. His voice was rumbling and careful, slow like a tortoise.

"Mr. Perry, Sasha needs something to eat."

"Well, lunch service is just about to start if you'll give me a moment to—"

"I'm sorry, but I need you to start serving right now. Lunch, or anything else you can put together on the quick. Look at this child!" Sasha stumbled slightly as Miss Islip pulled her forward. Mr. Perry drew back when he saw Sasha's shadowed face.

"It's no lie. That girl needs something to eat. Right away." Mr. Perry hustled to the kitchen while Miss Islip sat Sasha down at a table.

"Has your mom or dad bought food for your house, Sasha?" the teacher asked as she settled in across the table. "Do they cook for you? Tell me how I can help."

Sasha stared down at her hands in her lap. She inhaled and could smell the fragrant floral scents of the roses in the Cirque garden. She longed to be back there, not here, where Miss Islip's kind stare made Sasha feel as small as a rolled-up pill bug. She didn't need help. She *didn't.*

"I gathered this together real quick," Mr. Perry announced, coming out from behind the counter with a tray loaded with food. He set it down in front of Sasha with a flourish. "But I got a nice piece of roast turkey and some stuffing warming up too. Go on, child. Get started. Eat up."

Sasha stared at the food. A bowl of cut fruit. Carrot sticks and dip. A muffin. Two cartons of milk. She marveled that she didn't feel hungry anymore. All this food in front of her, but her eyes could do nothing more than glaze over, and her mouth could do nothing more than grimace. Mr. Ticklefar and Aunt Chanteuse had brought food for her and Toddy every single day since their parents had flown away. But guilt made Sasha refuse it. Even now she shrank away from the table and would have fallen to the floor had Miss Islip not jumped up, skittered around the table, and caught Sasha in her arms.

"Whoops, no falling over." Miss Islip put her arm around Sasha and pulled the girl close. Then, incapable of fighting the impulse, Miss Islip dashed a kiss onto the top of Sasha's head.

A shock of electricity, like one gets from flipping a

poorly wired light switch, came with the kiss. It stunned Sasha at first, then tingled over her scalp in the most luscious of zings and zaps. It washed over her neck and shoulders, down her arms, and to her thin fingertips. And it burst the dam in her eyes.

Tears rushed in like an eager spring river, filling and overflowing Sasha's lids. They gathered in the dark socket below her irises, filled the hollows in her cheeks, and seeped into the line between her lips.

Sasha ducked her head under Miss Islip's arm and shook, the sobs racking her body with shudders. Snot gathered in her nose, and she worried that her nostrils would clog up and suffocate her, but she hardly cared because she could be all right dying with the warmth that filled her heart right then.

But Sasha was not to die. The tears that couldn't stop and the arms that enfolded her and the kiss that she hadn't realized she had been aching for worked together to melt the adhesive that had bound her mouth shut. The glue dissolved, and it tickled her lips as it did so, as though hundreds of tiny butterflies were batting their gossamer wings against her skin.

Sasha laughed.

She laughed again, realizing what she could do. A grainy dryness filled her mouth, but she could open it. And she could laugh.

Miss Islip laughed. Mr. Perry did too, a growling sort of laugh that came more from his belly than his mouth.

"I'll leave you to it, then," he told them as he headed back to the kitchen. "And don't you feel shy 'bout saying hi to me from now on, Sasha. You just let me know when you're feeling peckish, hear?" Sasha nodded at his retreating back and turned her attention back to the food.

"It's like magic," she said slowly, tasting her words as though they were her first. "Talking again. Almost like the Light is back."

"Sometimes all the magic in the world can't solve our problems," Miss Islip said sadly. "But I'm glad you're speaking again. I want to hear all about what's going on at home." Miss Islip pressed her palm to her chest. "And what's going on in here."

Sasha nodded. She could tell Miss Islip about her parents being taken away easily enough, but to reveal the secrets of her heart was more difficult. She wasn't sure she knew all those secrets herself.

"But first you eat." The teacher sat up straight and tall. "You have to go slowly." She picked up the spoon and dipped it into the fruit. "Here. Take your time. One little bite at a time. I'm going to go get Tod. He'll need some lunch too."

"Oh, I made sure he was eating," Sasha whispered.

"I can tell you took care of him, but now . . ." Miss Islip hesitated, but she never finished her sentence. She only sighed gently. "Stay here and eat, and if anyone says anything to you, just call for Mr. Perry, understand?"

Sasha nodded again and took the utensil in her hand. She brought it to her lips, tasted the cold, fleshy sweetness of pear on her tongue, and sighed. Miss Islip's instructions stayed in her mind, though, and she ate as slowly as she could. The food was luxurious in her stomach, but it also hurt, like swallowing pine needles.

Or maybe that was just Miss Islip's kindness that hurt so much. A kindness Sasha knew she didn't deserve.

Chapter 15

The next morning Sasha watched Toddy tuck away more scraps of his breakfast.

"What *are* you doing with that food?" Sasha asked.

Toddy shrugged, but when they opened their front door to leave for school, a marbled gray creature darted under their legs and burrowed beneath the blanket on the sofa.

"Oh!" Toddy said. "He finally came in. I've been trying to convince him for days and days. It's hard for him to trust people."

"He who? *Toddy.*"

Sasha and Toddy crept to the couch, and each took a corner of the blanket. With one look at each other, they flipped it over to reveal a trembling kitten.

"Oh!" said Sasha.

"It's the one from the train tracks," Toddy explained. He knelt down and pulled the breakfast scraps from his pockets. "I've been feeding him. I hoped he would like me."

The kitten nuzzled Toddy's palm and licked the food slowly.

"I think it's working," Sasha said.

"I named him Pirate because he only has one good eye."

Sasha bit her lip. "Naming means keeping."

"I know," Toddy said in a small, hopeful voice.

"Cats catch birds, you know."

Toddy frowned. "Pirate wouldn't."

"How do you know?"

"He just wouldn't!"

Sasha nodded. She reached out a hand and was surprised when Pirate pushed his face right into her palm. The kitten's fur was even softer than she'd imagined. His purrs filled the room.

"You're good at taking care of animals," Sasha said.

Toddy picked Pirate up and cuddled him. "I know. That's because they let me help them."

All week Sasha and Toddy watched the skies for their parents' return and at the same time watched the

Cirque to see if anyone else disappeared.

"The Smoke is real settled," Aunt Chanteuse said one day, catching up with Sasha and Toddy outside the big tent. "Like it's gathering strength. I don't know what it's doing, but I don't trust it. The last time I saw Smoke was right before your mom arrived. It likes to sneak in when the Cirque's between Lights. But that was only a couple of days. Now . . ."

Griffin poked his head out of the tent. "Now everyone's just waiting for another Light to show up, and they're taking too long to get here. People are worried. But you know what I think? I think it's all nonsense and if we just stopped moaning about fairy tales and got back to work, we'd get everything back up and running in no time."

"Shush, boy," Aunt Chanteuse said.

But Griffin's words had hit home. Sasha squeezed Toddy's hand. Would her mom ever be able to come back to the Cirque if a new Light came to take her place? Why hadn't Sasha pointed the Smoke out to her mom when she'd had the chance? If only she had, the Cirque would be full of work and laughter and fun, like it was before. And Mom and Dad would still be around.

"Please come home," Sasha repeated to herself every day. She and Toddy watched and waited, and would have watched all day long, had Mr. Ticklefar not insisted they go to school.

"We can take care of you here until your parents come back," he said as he walked them to the bus stop one morning.

"Do you think they will?" Sasha said quickly.

"I believe! You know that. And you know we'll do whate'r we can for you. Yer family. But if you start missing out on yer schoolin', well, they'll send the people for you."

Sasha didn't know who "the people" were, but if they planned on taking her away from Cirque Magnifique, how would her parents know where to find her when they returned?

When the bus pulled up, Mr. Orner squinted at the circus ringmaster.

"Are you their dad?"

"No," Sasha said. "That's Mr. Ticklefar, the ringmaster. My mom and dad flew away and I don't know if they're coming back, but if they do, I need to stay at the Cirque so they know where to find me."

Mr. Orner squinted at Sasha but didn't say another word.

When Sasha dropped Toddy off in his classroom a few mornings later, Miss Islip stood by the window, gazing out over the courtyard.

"Good morning," she said when Sasha and Toddy stood next to her. "Wouldn't it be nice if someone planted a garden out there?"

Toddy scratched his head thoughtfully.

"The pixies would love that," Sasha said. "Daffodils and pansies and roses. And trees. And shrubs. And a little pebble path with mint that frogs could leap over."

Miss Islip smiled. "You seem to know a lot about gardening. Do you garden at home?"

Sasha shook her head.

"I just like flowers." Sasha waved good-bye to her brother and joined her own class.

At the close of the school day, Sasha went down the hall and around the corner to pick up Toddy as she always did. She slowed as she approached his classroom. Two figures stood in the hallway, arguing in fierce whispers.

The school principal, Mr. Rottenhammer, his bow tie askew and his pen leaking a dark blue puddle into his pants pocket, faced Miss Islip with an outstretched stack of paperwork.

"You can call Mrs. Flint at home to get help with them. And ask the other teachers in the room for help. But they need to be filled out by the end of the month."

"But that's less than two weeks away," Miss Islip protested. "And I've been working one-on-one with Tod for only a short time. 'What are his napping patterns? How many times per day, on average, does he ignore written rules?' I can't answer these. And maybe Mrs. Flint didn't tell you, but she and her broken hip went to visit her sister in Florida. I don't have that phone number."

"Miss Islip, I don't know what to tell you. Do the best you can. Nobody really cares how accurate the answers are anyway."

Miss Islip flinched as though Mr. Rottenhammer had struck her, but she sucked down her gasp and clutched her fists instead.

"No one cares? Well, I can believe that about this place. But what about this"—Miss Islip rattled the forms in her hand—"this Yarrowood School for Special Students? Do they care at all? Where are you sending him?"

Mr. Rottenhammer huffed angrily and poked his sharp, weaselly nose into Miss Islip's face. "*I'm* not sending the boy anywhere. Their parents are gone."

"Gone? Are you sure?" Miss Islip said.

"Quite sure. Ms. Terrywater hasn't been able to reach them. Then a couple mornings ago that Cirque man with the ridiculous mustache pretended to be their dad, to throw us off the scent, I suppose. But Mr. Orner alerted the state, as he is required to. The Yarrowood school is the county's request. The boy doesn't talk, and he needs to go someplace where he can be helped."

Mr. Rottenhammer pulled a handkerchief from the unstained pocket and mopped his shining brow. Sasha's little smile slipped out without permission; the way he was looking at Miss Islip was the same way he looked at Mrs. Flint. But with Miss Islip it was funny. And Miss Islip was not done with the principal just yet.

"I'm helping him *here*! Just look at this address! Have you noticed how far this place is from here? More than three hundred miles. You don't know where his parents are or when they'll get back. How will they know where to find him when they come home? And his sister? How will she see him? Toddy talks to her all the time—it makes no sense to take that away from him or her. What's she supposed to do? Where's she supposed to go?"

"I don't know," Mr. Rottenhammer murmured. "She'll be fine. I've seen the way she marches around here like she owns this whole school. She doesn't need anyone. And the boy needs someone with real expertise."

"And I suppose you don't care either, do you?" Miss Islip closed her eyes for a moment. Her palm rested over her rainbow pendant. "I know what it's like to have no one . . . no family, nothing." The teacher shook her head as if coming out of a trance, and frowned. "What if I don't think this is the best thing for Tod? What if I refuse to fill out the form?"

The rebellious tone of Miss Islip's words finally made Mr. Rottenhammer snap to attention, forgetting all about his handkerchief, which slipped from his fingers to the floor. He narrowed his bushy eyebrows and poked his finger in her face.

"This is not up to you. You do not get to decide where the child goes. You said yourself, you barely know the boy."

"But I—I mean—"

"And furthermore, I can find someone else not only to complete the forms, but also to do your job. Is that what you want? No? Good. Then I suggest you fill out the forms as best you can and get them back to me within the week." Mr. Rottenhammer reached for his handkerchief and jammed it back into his pocket. "If you are as concerned about the boy as you profess to be, I would imagine that you'd want to make sure his new school knows as much about him as you do. Wouldn't that be the best way to be certain they'll take care of him, Miss Islip?"

The teacher's shoulders sagged. "Yes," she whispered to the principal's back.

Mr. Rottenhammer was already marching away down the hall, ignoring Sasha, who quickly turned to once again face the art-covered bulletin board on the wall.

Miss Islip's fingers found the rainbow pendant again

and fiddled with it nervously. She read through a couple of the pages in her hands before she turned into her classroom with a sigh.

Sasha stood in the hallway a few minutes longer, nibbling her bottom lip. She needed to think. She needed a plan. No one could take Toddy away from her and the Cirque.

CHAPTER 16

Cirque Magnifique hadn't been the same since Sasha's parents had flown away. The glitter and sequins, once as bright and marvelous as geodes in the sun, were dull and gray. The shadows through the trees, once places for fairies to play games of hide-and-seek, sneered at Sasha. Bits of stone and dust trickled off the cottages here and there, and the tent poles were too bent to be used anymore.

With all the Cirque performances canceled, the Cirque folk were restless. More than one talked about leaving, about finding a new place to show their talents. Maybe across the sea or through the mountains. Somewhere the Magician's curse couldn't follow them.

"I heard of a place to the south . . . ," Sasha and

Toddy overhead one of the contortionist triplets say.

"You can't just *leave*." Sasha crossed her arms over her chest.

The contortionist frowned. "We can't just stay, either. Not when the Cirque—"

Aunt Chanteuse came up to Sasha and put her arms around the girl. "We all go wherever our song takes us. For some that's to the south. For Mr. Ticklefar, that's to all the corners of the earth. Others know it's their time and take their music to a new life."

"It's not time for the Cirque," Toddy whispered to Sasha. The words sent a shiver down her spine.

But Mr. Ticklefar remained stout too. He came to the cottage and knocked once, knowing Sasha wouldn't open the door for him, but he opened it anyway and shuffled into the entryway, pausing as if he weren't sure he should be there. The sleeves on his shirt were rolled up to his elbows, showing off his brown forearms. Rainbow suspenders—the old-fashioned kind—buttoned to his pants. In his fingers, tipped with mud-caked nails, he held a book and a piece of paper. Pirate hid under a chair, only his whiskers poking out curiously.

"You left this story in the dressing tent a while back. Thought you'd like to have it." Mr. Ticklefar came farther into the cottage and placed the book on a low table. "I was ne'er one to mince words," he said. He unfolded the paper and set it on top of the book. His voice caught, and he cleared his throat and tried again. "Them's papers from a place that wants to take Tod away."

Sasha's spoon clattered in her bowl. Mr. Perry had sent them home the day before with bags brimming with little boxes of cereal and cartons of milk, and they made a delightful dinner. But now the food caught in her throat. "What place? Is this because of the Magician? He can't. He won't. I won't let him take any more of my family!"

"Hurmph!" said Mr. Ticklefar. His eyes darted around the room, taking in the broken bike against the wall and the chipped mugs on the counter. The Brown family never had put much value on things. Still, there had always been a warm feeling in the room. As warm and cozy inside as it was cold and fearsome outside, as though it were the one place the Smoke couldn't get in. Until Sasha let it in. "The Magician does all sorts of squirrely things, and without a Light—"

"Why?" Sasha interrupted. "*Why* does he do this?"

Mr. Ticklefar removed his tall, velvet top hat and ran his hand over his bristly hair. He pointed to the sofa, and Sasha nodded. The ringmaster settled in, clearing his throat.

"Some folks think the Magician weren't always bad. Maybe not . . . maybe not. But there's a partic'lar darkness to men who believe they should have everything they want, and the Magician was one of them kinds. His is a terrible tale of love forlorn and hate newborn. I know you've heard bits and pieces o'er the years. Folks like to talk, and all. But maybe it's time . . . you hear it all. Many generations ago, a man fell in love with a woman . . ."

Sasha began to fall under the spell of a Mr. Ticklefar story. She sank into a cushion opposite the ringmaster. Her eyes glazed over as she began to see the world Mr. Ticklefar unraveled. Pirate tiptoed from beneath the chair and leaped to her lap, but hopped down again with a disgruntled mewl when Sasha couldn't be bothered to pet him.

"No one knows where, exactly, the Magician came from. Only that he found the Cirque, as so many with curious and extraordinary talents do. They say the Magician could call the very lightning of the sky to his hands," Mr. Ticklefar said. "My book o' lore says he burned down a tent accidentally once! But the real lightning were the moment Lilit walked into the Cirque. She was the most confident, kindest lady the Magician had e'er seen, and he loved her immediately. But Lilit saw something dark and vacuous in the depths of the Magician's soul. He courted her for years, but she could not love him back. Perhaps she knew he wanted her . . . the way he wanted audience admiration or beautiful jewels. It were a selfish kind of love. He was obsessed and, after a time, began to pull the life from her just as he pulled electricity from the clouds, that's how bad he wanted all the pieces of her. Pretty soon, there weren't hardly any life left in her.

"The Magician went to Lilit one last time as she were dyin'," Mr. Ticklefar continued. "'I will heal you,' he told her. 'You only must love me.' But she could not. Everyone else in the Cirque tried to nurse her back to health. But they also warned her to stay away from the Magician. Not as though she needed their words, mind you. Her smarts—brain and heart—were the stuff of legend. But so was the Magician's power. Their battle were silent, but fierce, and there couldn't be a true winner, understand? So instead of letting him take the last of her life, she rode her horse into the sea, transformed into an orca, and swam for the north seas, up near the Edge of the World, where she was never heard from again." Mr. Ticklefar's voice became softer. "The Magician blamed everyone but himself. He pulled all magic from the Cirque and channeled it into the Smoke, a dark, always lurking force that wants to take the life from the Cirque forever. That's when the Great Therianthropy happened. You know what that is?"

Sasha dropped her eyes to her lap. The Great Therianthropy was something talked about in hushed voices, and never to children. Sasha herself knew so much about it only because she'd snuck in and read that old book of lore in Mr. Ticklefar's dressing room, when she'd gone in to look for him that one time. The door had been open a smidge, and a voice—she was sure there had been a voice, one she'd thought was Mr. Ticklefar's—had invited her in. So she'd entered.

The ringmaster had been gone, but on the table beneath the great mirror, an old-looking book had lain open. Sasha hadn't been able to help but read. She'd always been so curious. And the pictures of the Great Therianthropy—the contorted bodies and screaming children and destruction of everything so that all that was left was windswept dirt—had held her eyes to the page.

She'd learned about the terrible things that had happened the first time the Smoke had engulfed the Cirque. And she had sounded out that big word—the-ree-an-throw-pea—so many times under her breath that she could say it as easily as her own name. It had terrified her, that word, and she'd wanted to repeat it until she owned it. Until she could take apart all the pieces that scared her and toss them to the wind. Until the syllables were meaningless letters and nothing more.

She didn't tell Mr. Ticklefar she'd seen those terrible drawings in his book of lore—the most awful being the all-seeing eyes of the Magician himself—but he seemed to know she'd looked.

"It ain't a thing we talk about, but Cirque folks . . . we

know, don't we? After that the Magician fled to the Edge of the World, where he waits for us all to be destroyed."

Mr. Ticklefar leaned forward and lowered his voice to a whisper. "Sometimes, Sasha, when a person is hurt in their very core, they want everyone around them to hurt too."

Sasha blinked, and the spell of Mr. Ticklefar's story was broken. Her insides squirmed with an emotion she couldn't—or maybe didn't want to—name.

Mr. Ticklefar sighed and stood. "Anyway, it's not the Magician splitting the two of you up. It's Islanders."

Sasha let out a slow breath. Was there a difference?

"I'm not sure there's anything we can do to stop them. Me an' Aunt Chanteuse are doin' our best to take care of you, but we're not yer parents. We got no 'thority."

"They're not taking my brother!" Sasha nibbled on her fingernails. "We can stop them. Of course we can. If we defeat the Smoke, then Mom and Dad will come back and no one will take Toddy anywhere. And then we can rebuild the Cirque. We have to find the Magician and convince him to lift the curse!"

Mr. Ticklefar twirled his mustache.

"Last I heard he was living at the Edge of the World. But, girl, I been all over the planet, from east to west and top to bottom. I been in caverns about the size of your thumb and wastelands that went on as far as you could see. I've traipsed in deserts and sailed across seas. I ain't never seen the likes of that nasty Magician. I don't right believe he lives anymore."

"He has to," Sasha insisted. "Or else the curse would have died too."

They all knew Sasha was right. And there the Smoke was, rising and falling outside like a slowly breathing cover of mist. Suffocating them all.

"I'm going to find the Magician. Me and Toddy both are." Sasha's eyes shone as she spoke, as though a little bit of the magic that filled Toddy was suddenly a part of her, too.

Mr. Ticklefar sighed. Sasha bristled. He didn't believe she could do it, find the Magician and bring Light back to the Cirque.

But it was her fault the Smoke was taking over.

She had to save everything. She just had to.

Mr. Ticklefar reached into his pocket and pulled out a small brown bag tied with a string. "I don't got much. I never were a man for collecting things. But I got something for you, because you never know when you're going to need to fix your own things." He passed the bag to Sasha.

She untied the bag and poured the contents into her hand. "It's a seed," she said.

"I got it in the jungle," Mr. Ticklefar said. "From a man

who was there one second and gone the next. I never got his name. But he gave me this and said a few important things with his eyes—not his mouth, mind you, his eyes, sorta like your brother's eyes just now—and went away again. I was saving it up for . . . well . . . I ain't sure what I was saving it up for, but a moment like this and a girl like you feels just about right somehow."

Sasha rolled the seed around in her palm. Doubt crept in. It was just a seed. Nothing more. Nothing that would help her find the Magician. "We're supposed to plant it? It's too cold outside." Sasha wasn't a great gardener, but she at least knew that flowers didn't grow in the winter. "It won't grow."

Mr. Ticklefar harrumphed. "This is a fine time for planting a seed like this one, I think. Find the right spot for it, though. Not too much shade, but not too much light. Jungle light: a little here, a little there. I ain't a gardener, but this looks like a seed that needs just the right amount of light. That, good island soil, and some water should do it." Mr. Ticklefar stood and brushed off his pant legs. "Time to be off to bed. By the looks of the sky, you should too. It's best if we're well tucked in and safe, at night." He glanced out the window at the growing Smoke. Sasha was certain any amount of danger could be hiding in its gray thickness.

Mr. Ticklefar's fingers rolled the brim of his hat back

and forth, mulling over one last thing he needed to say. “Sasha, I can’t be a hundred percent sure yer mom and dad . . .” The ringmaster swallowed. “Maybe . . . uh . . . I’ll send Aunt Chanteuse over. She’s a touch better at . . . these things.”

Mr. Ticklefar retreated and closed the cottage door softly behind him.

Sasha glanced at her little brother. She couldn’t imagine the cottage without him. It would be too big, too lonely. Who would leave strange-critter stuffed animals lying everywhere? And eat big bowls of cereal with her, them stuffing their bellies with flakes until they could hardly move? And who would walk with her to the bus stop, helping her feel courageous, like she could take on a whole school of the Islanders no matter how much they bullied and made fun of the Cirque kids? She simply couldn’t be without him. And he certainly couldn’t be without her.

And they both needed their parents.

Why did she have to be so awful?

Sasha and Toddy watched Mr. Ticklefar out the window until his form disappeared like a ghost in the night. Then they went to their room. They slipped into bed. In the silence of evening they could hear the gentle whipping of the Cirque tents. Pirate pattered in between them. He went to Toddy first, nuzzling the boy’s nose. He turned to Sasha.

She gazed at the kitten. His single good eye was pale green, and she could almost see through it.

"What do you think about, Pirate?" Sasha said.

Toddy stroked the kitten's tail. "He's wondering if he should be scared of you."

"Of me? I'm not scary."

Toddy hummed. Pirate stalked back and forth over the bed until, finally, he curled into a ball against Sasha's chest. She couldn't help but grin, and Toddy matched her toothy smile. But then he frowned.

"Are we going to different homes?" Toddy asked.

Sasha shook her head and tightened her grip on her brother's hand. A lazy nighttime shower pitter-pattered on the roof. "I won't let him—anyone—do that."

Sasha rolled the bag with the seed around in one palm. It felt like there was another seed lodged in her throat as she thought about how not only had she sent Mom and Dad away, but now people wanted to take Toddy. And it was all her fault.

She didn't know how long paperwork took, but she had a feeling there wasn't much time for them to find the Magician and lift the curse and get Mom and Dad back. She had to make some big decisions, and make them fast.

Or else Toddy would be taken away forever.

CHAPTER 17

Before school the next morning Toddy traipsed through the Cirque grounds, searching for the best place to plant the seed. It seemed every inch of the grounds was occupied by a tent or equipment or another plant or tree or vegetable patch, and no space to be made for a new specimen.

"What about the side of the cottage?" Sasha joined her brother, gazing nervously at the brightening sky. "But we have to hurry."

"I don't like the tower." Toddy squinted up at the old water tower in the distance, an oversize wooden barrel on rusted iron legs to the south of the Cirque grounds. It looked like a strong wind could blow it right over, despite having stood its ground through many island squalls.

"It's too far away to fall on anything by us. It'll be okay. There's an open spot here that should get the right amount of sun."

"What if it doesn't grow here?" Toddy asked, opening his fist and eyeing the scattered patches of grass where Sasha pointed.

"We're supposed to plant it in the light. And the shade. And this looks about right."

Toddy studied the long shadows of the cottage blanketing the planting space, then gazed at the sky, calculating. Then he looked back at his sister and nodded. Sasha shrugged. She was trying to be brave for her brother, but deep down she didn't think planting a seed was going to change anything.

"It should grow," she said. "Mr. Ticklefar said so. I'll dig a hole, and you get some water."

Toddy scrutinized the seed. It was the size of a peach pit but perfectly smooth, marbled green-and-white like a jade dragon's egg.

With a sigh Toddy passed the seed to his sister and went for a bucket of water. Sasha fell to her knees and worked at the ground with her fingers. The dirt was moist and soft but packed together by stubborn grass roots and wind and rain, and worms came to the surface to see who was disturbing their tunnels. A spindly-legged spider crawled over her fingers like they were bridges, and pill bugs scurried in the opposite direction as she pulled clumps of soil from the ground. When Toddy returned with the water, he got down next to his sister and worked with her.

When they had dug a hole the size of a salad bowl, Toddy dropped the seed in. They covered it and patted the dirt into place. Sasha poured the bucket of water over the area, and they watched the soil turn black with wetness.

"How long will it take?" Toddy asked.

Sasha shrugged. "I don't know. But we should check on it every day. And not forget to water it either, in case it's not raining."

"It's always raining," Toddy said.

"Then that makes our job easier." Sasha stood and brushed her hands on her skirt. "We better get going or we'll miss the bus."

Sasha and Toddy dashed down the hill, racing like birds on a downwind, and then slowed to a careful walk once they were near the bus stop. Shelby and Griffin were there, crunching tall grass under their boots.

"Pretty wet, huh?" Shelby said, squinting at the gray sky. The sun had disappeared for the season, and now a light mist muted all the colors on the island, so that everything looked like an old-fashioned photograph.

"How are you doing?" Shelby asked. "Especially since—"

"Fine," Sasha blurted out.

Shelby exchanged a glance with her brother. Griffin shrugged.

"I heard the kids at school are being a little . . . mean." Shelby reached out for a hug, but Sasha shrank away.

"It's not just you," Griffin said. "Islanders don't like any Cirque kids. Except me."

"Griffin, shut up," Shelby snapped. "I've heard you say mean things about the Cirque to the Islanders. We're not all two-faced like you are."

"Yeah, well, I defend the Cirque too. Nobody's perfect on this island."

Sasha studied the older boy. His eyes were hooded, and his lower lip jutted out a tiny bit, so that he always looked petulant. When he was at the Cirque, he seemed to love it. He had a particular talent for lighting and staging. But when he was away, he acted relieved to leave it all behind. In some ways Sasha understood. If it meant she could have Islander friends like Griffin did, she might pretend all the Cirque lore was lies too. Except . . .

"Where do you think my parents went, then?" Sasha whispered.

Griffin watched her, swallowing. "They call things the Smoke, but it's really just fog, don't you see? Everything has a simple answer."

"But . . . ," Sasha began again.

"Your dad's accident was terrible." Griffin looked at the ground. He was saved from elaborating further by the arrival of his school bus. Not long after, the elementary school bus pulled up too.

When they got on and sat in their seats, Kirk Stoddard leaned over and looked at Sasha's hands. "Look at you, filthy Cirque freaks."

Sasha stared at her fingernails, caked with mud, while her cheeks burned with shame. "We're not filthy."

"We're not filthy," Kirk mocked. He turned back around and laughed with his friends.

Toddy whispered to Sasha: "What if we can't find Mom and Dad and no one wants us because we're filthy?"

"We're not filthy. Besides, they'll always want you because you're magic—" Sasha bit her tongue before she could say the rest of what she knew to be true in her heart: that Toddy himself was a Light. Certainly he was *her* Light, and probably the very Light needed to save the Cirque. Sasha didn't know all the strange magic of how and when Lights were revealed—her mom had simply appeared one day because she felt a pull, and Cirque lore mentioned other Lights who simply stood tall when they knew it was their time—but if she told everyone Toddy was a Light, did that mean her mom and dad would be lost to them forever? She wouldn't let the Cirque replace her mom, and so Sasha tucked her secret knowledge deep down and shook her head. "You're wonderful and I'm . . ."

Her gaze traveled over her worn shoes; her skinny, bruised, and mud-caked legs; her dress, unraveling at the seams. She reached her hands to her forehead, and wanted to pull, pull, pull on her unevenly chopped bangs until the hurt on her head was bigger than the hurt in her heart. Her tongue searched but couldn't find the right word to describe herself. There was no word for her, nothing terrible enough for a child that no one wanted. A child so awful that she would tell her own mother that she didn't want to be with her.

Sasha shook her head. "They're going to come back, Toddy. I know they will. We'll find the Magician and banish the Smoke, and everything will go back to the way it was."

CHAPTER 18

The mist continued all through recess. Half of Sasha's class stayed huddled near the school doors, glaring at the rain. Miss Islip had brought Toddy outside to play, but Mr. Rottenhammer called her back inside for a meeting. Miss Islip had a brief word with the fifth-grade teacher on recess duty that week before slipping back inside the building.

"Let's go look for pretty rocks in that pile," Sasha said, pointing to a spot not far from the blacktop, where the boys in her class played a ruthless game of tag.

"Okay," Toddy replied. "I'm going to find one to put in a king's crown."

The two settled into the grass and busied themselves with picking through the pile and polishing the rocks with the nicest colors. They were so involved in their work that they didn't hear their schoolmates approaching them. Long shadows settled over the ground like thunderclouds.

"Whacha up to, Sausage Brown?" Kirk sneered. His friends laughed.

"Searching for jewels," Sasha said, squinting up at Jenny Myers. "Do you want to find some?"

Jenny Myers sucked on her lip. Sasha's heart raced. There were a hundred reasons why Sasha didn't want to go to school, but there were also one or two reasons why she did. The hope of making a friend out of Jenny Myers was one. And for a second it seemed that Jenny was really going to sit down and sort rocks with her. If she did, Sasha knew they would find two sparkling stones and, with them, make two crowns, twisting like vine tendrils. They would be the most wonderful queens the Cirque had ever seen.

But then Jenny glanced at Kirk. Her shoulders slumped and she lowered her head, shaking it slowly.

Kirk smirked. "Jenny doesn't play with girls like you."

"Why not?"

"You smell and you're ugly and your brother is stupid and you don't even know it."

Sasha clenched her fists. She was not a pretty girl, she knew. But that didn't matter. Kirk Stoddard had said something mean about Toddy.

"He is not stupid!"

Jenny looked up, and Sasha clamped her lips together. Yelling at someone never made Sasha want to be that person's friend, so why would a person want to be hollered at? And Jenny was the one person Sasha wanted to be her friend. Ever since the first day of school. There was something about the way Jenny caught Sasha's eye sometimes, in class. Like she wanted to say something nice but couldn't. Sasha took a slow breath. "He's wonderful. Magical."

"I think he is too," Jenny whispered.

The other kids around them snorted like hogs.

Kirk reached over and tugged Sasha's hair, then yanked the rocks from her hand. Toddy made an angry noise.

"Gurgle, gurgle, gurgle," Colton mimicked, flapping his arms around like a panicked bird.

"Give those back," Sasha yelled. She stood, pebbles falling from her lap, and shoved one hand into Kirk's chest.

Kirk and Colton and the rest of the boys and girls went silent. Not the calm kind of silent but the dangerous kind. Sasha took a step backward, crushing rocks under the heel of her shoe.

"Sausage here thinks she's the toughest of us all," Kirk said.

"She ain't nothing," Colton put in.

"No, she ain't," Kirk said, sticking his face right into Sasha's. "She ain't like us. You wanna be like us? You and your dumb brother? And your dead dad and mom? I bet they were glad to get away from you two. I can't blame them."

"They're not dead! They flew away into the sky and are waiting for us to defeat the Magician and save them!"

Kirk shoved Sasha in the shoulder. "She's as stupid as her brother."

Sasha threw her whole body at Kirk, pushing her hands up toward Kirk's smug smile. She didn't care if Mrs. Porter, the teacher on recess duty, saw her fighting. She only cared about getting Kirk away from Toddy.

Kirk lost his balance, but recovered quickly. He shoved Sasha back to the ground with one vicious thrust. Colton grabbed Toddy, pulling the younger boy's arms behind his back.

Sasha jumped up. "Get off of him!"

Kirk shoved her again, and Sasha tumbled to the blacktop. She rubbed the back of her head and glared at Kirk when he pressed his boot onto her stomach.

"Don't you get it? We don't want your kind here."

"It's not only *your* school," Sasha gasped.

"You guys hurry it up," Colton said. "This kid's wriggly."

A pair of feet clacked on the blacktop; Sasha looked up to see Jenny dashing away from them. Sasha's heart dropped. Jenny wouldn't even help defend her and Toddy. It was ridiculous to have ever hoped Jenny would be her friend.

"Shut up, Markson," Kirk called back. Then he removed his boot with a smile. "Ah, Sausage, don't worry. We're just havin' fun. Here, want help up?" Kirk held out his hand like a peace offering. Sasha took it warily and was hauled to her feet just long enough to see the glint of menace flash in Kirk's eye.

"No!" she screamed, feeling his grip tighten on hers. He spun her around so that her back was to his front and shoved her to the ground.

Sasha fell to her knees, the skin around the caps ripping like a seam on a skirt. Someone else hauled her back up again and pushed, tossing her like a rag doll to the blacktop once more. The biting in her knees quickened. Pain prickled up her thighs. Tears gathered in the corners of her eyes. Her knees took on the ugly color of blacktop dirt and glossy red finger paint.

Screaming and crying and laughter all mingled together around her ears like the swirling of a tornado. She couldn't pick the sounds apart, figure out which voice was hers. It wasn't until the bell cut through their voices that the laughter ended. Colton released Toddy, and all the other kids ran into the school. Sasha limped after them slowly, staring at the blacktop through watery eyes. When she reached the door, Kirk Stoddard blocked it with his arms and legs.

"No freaks past this point," he said.

"We have to go in too," Sasha said. "Let us in."

Kirk shook his head. "Go back to where you came from."

Colton swore. "Porter's coming. Move!"

Kirk squinted at the two figures coming toward them. "That Jenny who got her?"

Colton cussed again. "I'll deal with her later."

Kirk slammed the door in Sasha's face, and the boys ran off. Mrs. Porter rushed down the hall after them.

Only Jenny remained. Toddy locked eyes with her through the glass. For a moment Sasha thought Toddy was going to say something to Jenny. Sasha waited and watched, but only a silent communication passed between them. Jenny pushed the door open slowly and reached her hand to Toddy, then pulled him gently into the school. She saw Sasha's bloody knees and winced.

"They're so mean. Are you okay?" Jenny looked surprised that she had dared ask the question. She didn't wait for Sasha to answer before whirling around and dashing back to the classroom.

"It's all right, Toddy." Sasha drew herself up, wincing

at the stinging in her legs. She gasped in a breath of air and wiped her face with the back of her hand. "Mrs. Porter will take care of it."

Sasha didn't believe her own words, but she sighed and pressed the hem of her skirt to the ugly scrapes on her knees. Blood seeped into the fabric and darkened the brown weave in two round spots. Sasha sucked air through her front teeth and tried not to scream again, then turned her skirt from front to back. She didn't want anyone to notice her injuries.

Miss Islip hurried down the hallway toward them. She crouched in front of Sasha, her eyes heavy with sadness.

"It's okay," Sasha said again, before Miss Islip could speak. "I just need to get my mom and dad."

"Wait, Sasha. Your mom is back? What do you mean? Let's call her."

"No, she's still . . . It's just that they . . . turned into birds and—" Sasha made a flapping motion in the air with her arms.

"Sasha . . . they couldn't do that. It's not possible. Listen. I know what it's like to be left alone. My parents died when I was little. I have no brothers or sisters. I'm the last of my kind." Miss Islip gave a sad little laugh. "I might know a little of how you feel right now. I spent years make-believing my parents were still around too. But I think if we find you the right home, one full of kindness, we can find you happiness here, in the real world." Miss Islip's voice was so gentle that Sasha wasn't mad at her for not believing her parents were birds. Just sad. "But the truth is," Miss Islip continued, "nothing is that easy."

Sasha blinked at Miss Islip. "They did turn into birds. Promise. But we're fine. *We* are taking care of us."

"If I could make the world different for you two, I would." Miss Islip blinked back at Sasha and drew Toddy in close, wrapping her arms around him in a hug. "I know you don't understand now, but someday I hope you will. Magic is all well and good, but . . . real life is something different. I'm going to see if you can come home with me tonight."

A shiver zinged up Sasha's back at the thought of staying overnight on the Islander side.

"We haven't been alone very long. A few weeks—*days*," she corrected as Miss Islip's face became even more concerned. "The Smoke makes it difficult to remember. But we're going to find the Magician and banish the Smoke, and everything will go back to normal."

Miss Islip drew her hand slowly across her forehead as she regarded the children. Her fingers twitched. Worry rose in Sasha as she watched Miss Islip. The teacher seemed dizzy, and her cheeks had gone paper white, like she really needed to lie down.

"Miss Islip . . ."

"Sasha, go on to class. You don't want to be late."

Miss Islip guided Toddy into his classroom, and Sasha hurried down the hallway and slipped into her own classroom just as the late bell sounded.

Ms. Terrywater met Sasha at her desk. There was disapproval in her face, and she looked from Sasha to the boys and back again. "Could you please tell someone at the Cirque to call me?"

"I'll try, but none of us talk very much, ever since the Smoke came."

"The Smoke?"

Sasha sighed. It was irritating that she had to explain about the Smoke over and over again.

"Yes. It came because of me, but it got so much worse after Mom and Dad turned into birds and flew away."

Ms. Terrywater placed a hand on Sasha's shoulder briefly, then walked back to her desk, picked up her phone, and dialed.

A sardonic "Oh my gosh" came from behind Sasha.

Across the aisle Colton laughed.

"Your mom and dad are birds?" Kirk Stoddard said, snipping at a corner of paper with his scissors. "Why do people even pay attention to you? You're a waste of space."

Sasha sucked on her lip. There were times when

she wanted nothing more than for Kirk Stoddard to get exactly what he deserved. But what that was, she didn't know. To feel the dark, little way she did when he was around? But there also was a conviction inside her that she didn't want to treat others the way he treated people. Even if he deserved it. Perhaps that made her a coward, or perhaps that made her something else, something better. Sasha had been on the wrong end of hurtful things for so long that maybe it would make her feel better to hurt them back. But she was also beginning to realize that even when it wasn't her fault, she got in trouble for everything. So what did *anything* matter?

"They could have," a voice pushed into the conversation. "Turned into birds."

Jenny Myers turned in her seat to give Kirk and Colton a shrewd look. As if daring them to challenge her.

"My gran told me about it. When she forbade me to ever set foot on that side of the island. She said Cirque people turn into animals when it's time to leave the island. Like reincarnation or something. And hundreds of years ago or something like that, it happened all at once. Everyone over there turned into animals and just disappeared. Because of a *curse*."

Jenny gave the boys a little smile, a creepy sort of look that made her eyes suddenly darker and her hair look like molten brass swirling hotly around her face.

"A bad old Magician cursed them to *die.* Every last one. The old people and the little kids, too. And when the Cirque was gone, everything on the island got bad. The docks shut down, and the shops and cafés. Because people didn't come here anymore. Gran said people started hating the Cirque not just because they were freaks. They ruined the townspeople's lives when they all disappeared. If you ask me, I think the worst thing was that all those people were there one day, and the next day just"—Jenny snapped her fingers—"gone."

Sasha squirmed. It didn't feel right, hearing her people's story being told by an outsider.

"Anyway," Jenny was saying, "my point is that the Cirque people *do* turn into animals. At least that's what Gran said, and my gran is the most honest person I know. More honest than your parents at least, Kirk Stoddard. *Gran* would never lie about being the ones who hit the eagle statue in front of town hall with their car like your dad and mom. And I don't think Sasha would either. So stop calling her a liar." Jenny hardly looked at Sasha, but even so, Sasha felt a bit of the pinched feeling in her stomach and spine subside.

Kirk Stoddard folded his arms and sulked. "I never called her a liar."

Jenny clucked her tongue and faced the front of

the room again with the air of someone who had won a great battle.

"We came back," Sasha said in a low voice.

Jenny turned around. "What?"

"You can't scrub a place of its magic. The Cirque . . . it was always waiting for its people to find it. We came back, and we're here now."

"My gran said that, too," Jenny said. "Cirque people started coming back when she was a teenager."

"I wish you'd go away for good," Kirk Stoddard muttered.

When Ms. Terrywater hung up the phone, she kept her back to the classroom for a moment, before walking to Sasha. "There are people on their way for you," she said. "Don't be scared; you're not in trouble. They're going to help take care of you for a little while."

Kirk laughed. "My wish came true."

Sasha gave a panicked jerk. "They're coming to take Toddy away?"

"You'll both go to good places, just for now, and then—"

"You're not taking Toddy away!" Sasha screamed. She flew at Ms. Terrywater, catching the teacher off guard, and pushed her into Kirk's desk.

"Sasha!"

"NO! STOP TRYING TO TAKE HIM AWAY!"

Sasha fled. She grabbed Toddy from his classroom without a word to Miss Islip, and they ran down the hall as fast as possible. They avoided the school's main entrance, where the office was, and darted through an open side door. Sprinting across the blacktop, Sasha and Toddy ignored the calls after them. They ran until their sides ached, until the bottoms of their feet hurt, until their lungs burned.

"They won't take you away," Sasha panted. "Never, ever." She fought back tears. She hobbled as she walked, moving through town in a daze of confusion and pain.

This side of the island was tidy. Shop windows sparkled beneath white, wooden trim. The sidewalks were swept clean, and the houses had little square lawns in fluorescent shades of green. What would it be like to live over here? There would be no smell of hay and horses. No trickling trails of glitter fallen off costumes. No black silk ringmaster's tent covered in constellations so that it seemed to be a vacuum of space and universes.

Definitely no Mom and Dad.

The thought frightened Sasha enough that she quickened her pace. She and Toddy raced away from town, across the train tracks, and back to Cirque land.

When they reached their cottage, Sasha and Toddy sprawled on the ground next to their seed, catching their breath.

"Where is our home, Toddy?" Sasha whispered.

"Here, at the Cirque." Pirate poked his head around the back of the cottage, and Toddy held out his hand. The kitten scampered to him and nuzzled Toddy's neck.

"What if they take us away? Then where's our home?" Sasha asked.

Toddy reached for his sister's hand. "Wherever you and Mom and Dad are is home."

Sasha brushed her hand across her face and reached over to pat Pirate.

They stared at molten marshmallow clouds, saying nothing more. Until the ground started to tremble. Pirate meowed indignantly, and Sasha sat up.

"What was that?"

Another rumble came from that bare, brown spot where they'd planted their seed. Like magic, a family of wiggling sprouts suddenly poked out from the top crust of the earth.

"It's growing!" Toddy grinned.

The clouds turned iron gray, and a few timid drops of rain fell onto their heads. But Sasha and Toddy stayed beside their new plant, even when the skies opened and drenched them.

As the afternoon wore on, their faces stung from the now heavy rain battering down on them. Still, they stayed to watch the sprouts turn into baby plants and post their first leaves. Sasha and Toddy built castle walls around the plants with rocks brought in from the train tracks and stood guard against the deer that poked their heads out from the forest, hoping for a nibble of tender new-plant. Pirate swiped away twilight slugs.

As night settled in, a bulb formed on one of the plants, but almost as soon as it appeared, the Smoke rolled in to cover the land so thickly that Sasha and Toddy lost sight of the bulb.

"We'd better go inside," Sasha said. The wind that came with the Smoke sounded like tremulous screams, and the cold made her very bones shiver. But tucked inside the cottage, all was warm and cozy again. Sasha gingerly washed her knees, and she and Toddy crawled into their pajamas, then into bed, Pirate purring between them. Sasha pulled out the book she'd started weeks ago but had tossed into the corner of the dressing room, unfinished. She opened to the bookmarked page and—

"Oh!"

A square of cardstock fell out. *You Are Invited to a Sleepover.*

How had it gotten there? When had it been put there? Sasha's mind reeled. The book had been with Sasha at school the day the invitations were handed out. It was that evening she'd tossed the book aside. Had

Jenny slipped it between the pages when Sasha wasn't looking? What might have changed, that night, had Sasha only known the invitation was there? She read the invitation through a dozen times at least, and then tucked it away and read five pages to Toddy, before they fell asleep to the song of each other's soft snores.

At the first light of day, they went to check on their plant. They both ground to a halt.

"Sasha," Toddy whispered. "I asked for a tree for Mommy and Daddy to build a nest in."

"What?"

"When we planted it."

They inched toward the place where they had planted Mr. Ticklefar's strange seed. Sasha reached for Toddy's hand and squeezed it. "It's not a tree," she breathed. "It's a boat."

CHAPTER 19

The bulb had burst. The bulb that Sasha, only the day before, had smiled over and secretly imagined becoming a flower bigger than her head, had opened while they'd been asleep. And inside the firm, shiny green capsule was not a pink daisy or a white orchid. It was a boat. And a big one too. Taller than the cottage itself, with billowing white sails that reached up into the sky and dark wood polished so hard that it gleamed like a flash of lightning.

"A boat," Sasha repeated in awe.

"A ship," Toddy said, feeling pleased to be able to correct his big sister. "Maybe even a pirate ship. Pirate! Is this your ship?" The kitten poked his head out the window and meowed dismissively before returning to his food bowl.

Sasha gave her brother a sidelong glance. "Pirates? Maybe we shouldn't go in, then." They looked at each other for a moment, then burst into laughter. "Race you!"

Sasha took off, leaving Toddy to catch up. She forgot about her skinned knees long enough to make it to the ladder that touched down on the soil, and began climbing. Toddy was right on her heels.

"I get to steer!" Toddy shouted up to her.

"You're too small!" Sasha hollered back down.

"Am not!"

"Besides, I'm older."

"So what? S'not fair!"

They scrambled onto the deck and tore up and down the gleaming wood planks. Sasha peered at her reflection in the shining brass accents while Toddy climbed the shrouds that led to the crow's nest and brandished an imaginary sword.

"Arr!" he growled to a flock of birds flying overhead.

Sasha hightailed it toward the highest point on middeck and, once she'd reached it, stood, staring at the monstrous wooden helm before her. The tip of her head just barely poked over the top of it, and it was as wide as her arms were, stretched out full. The wood, like the rest of the ship, was dark and beautifully grained. She reached a hand out and touched one of the spokes of the wheel and pulled.

Suddenly a wild gust of wind lifted Sasha's hair from the back of her neck. Her shirt flapped against her stomach as she fought to keep balance against the sudden, roaring gales. Smoke came up and swirled around the deck. Sasha's heart tightened.

"Come down!" Sasha screamed to Toddy. Her words blew away long before they could reach the crow's nest. The sails whipped and snapped and cracked. "Toddy!"

Toddy cried out in surprise as the ship lurched to the left with an echoing creak. He threw his arms around the mast and held on for his life. Sasha grasped at the wheel, trying to hold herself up as her feet went flying out from beneath her. The sudden windstorm rapidly grew in strength, rattling the fabric of the Cirque tents and the branches of the trees and shrubs in the garden; sequins, torn from the sparkling Cirque marquees, raced through the air and littered the top deck like confetti.

From the south an echoing growl rose to become a splintering roar.

"Sasha!" Toddy hollered, pointing with the hand that wasn't gripping the crow's nest basket.

In the distance the old water tower swayed under

the strength of the wind. It leaned to the side slowly, the round top inching closer to the ground. For a moment the wind stopped and the world waited in silent anticipation. Then a gust stronger than any before tore through the ship, knocking Sasha to her sore knees.

As she scrambled to her feet, a massive crash sounded from the distance. Just as her head rose above the railing of the ship, the water tower toppled over, smashing itself against the island and releasing a sea-size tidal wave toward their ship.

Sasha returned to the wheel, wrapped her arms around it, and held on as tightly as she could as the gales shoved at her. The water was coming at them fast. "Don't let go, Toddy!"

"But, Sasha!"

Sasha looked up. Her brother pointed to a spot on the ground just outside the ship. His face streamed with tears.

Sasha let go of the wheel and leaped. Her hands scrambled for the deck railing. She fell a few feet down the side of the ship before her hands wrapped around the wood and she was able to pull herself up the steps to the ship's forecastle. A mewl reached her on the wind. Sasha peeked overboard.

Pirate cried up to her. Sasha reached her arm down, but the kitten was too far away.

The wave roared down the slight valley between the Cirque tents and the cottages, hitting the ship and nothing else. Sasha lurched into the railing, her chest pressing painfully against the wood. The ship twisted and groaned.

Sasha gritted her teeth and fell to her hands and knees. She crept across the forecastle, descended to the main deck, and pulled herself up, midship. The wheel spun until it was a blur. Sasha knew if she tried to grab it, it might rip her arm off.

Something heavy slammed into her back, knocking Sasha forward. "Oof!"

When she looked up, a tree branch was rolling away from her.

"No, you don't!" She grabbed the branch, turned, and jammed it into the wheel. Wood creaked, splinters flew, and Sasha was flung across the deck.

But the branch held. For now. The wood bent as the ship fought against it. Sasha scrambled back to the wheel and used all the strength she had in her arms to keep the wheel from spinning out of control again. The ship rose and dove under the movement of the water. It didn't seem possible that the tower could have held so much; it was enough to make a small ocean. The water drowned the grasses in its narrow path. Sea salt splashed against the sides of the ship, spewing droplets into Sasha's hair.

Sasha licked her lips, surprised to taste salt.

"The ocean!" Sasha yelled up to Toddy.

She didn't know if the island was sinking, or the seas had risen, but it was impossible to look. In that moment, all Sasha could do was hold on tight and hope to not fall overboard. Soon enough the ship began to settle, floating steadily on the water and calming into a gentle rhythm as the winds subsided.

"Are you okay?" Sasha called up to the masts.

"I'm okay," Toddy said with a shaky voice. His eyes widened. He slid down the pole and ran to the edge of the deck to lean over the railing. When the ship tipped to one side, he reached down, and then straightened up again, a waterlogged creature purring in his arms. Toddy beamed. "You're a good swimmer for a cat."

"Pirate!" Sasha grinned and scratched the kitten behind one ear.

Pirate gave her a reproachful look but a moment later nudged her palm, deciding to forgive her short human arms.

Sasha scrutinized the helm and climbed a few steps to check the forecastle. Satisfied that the ship wasn't damaged, she returned to midship, reached a trembling finger to the wheel again, and gave it the teeniest of pushes. The ship swayed gently beneath her. She walked to the edge of the ship and looked overboard.

The ocean was blue and clear, except for a few pieces of splintered water tower. Their island was far in the distance; the Cirque was nowhere to be seen.

"We have to turn this thing around," she said. "We're going to get lost at sea."

Toddy joined her to watch the island grow smaller and smaller on the horizon.

"Or . . ." Sasha bit her bottom lip. The thing she wanted to do, the very brave and adventurous thing, was to go to the Edge of the World to find the old Magician and destroy the Smoke for good. But she wasn't sure she was ready.

Except, if not now, when? After Toddy was taken away from her? After she was taken from the Cirque? Mom and Dad were already gone, and there was nothing left to do but find them.

"Let's get rid of the Smoke, Toddy."

Toddy petted Pirate and didn't answer for a moment, but just at the point when Sasha had decided to spin the wheel again, he called out: "All right, Sasha. Let's go. But I want to drive!"

CHAPTER 20

They sailed for many days. Sasha let Toddy steer, but in the end Toddy preferred scaling the masts and exploring the floors belowdecks. So Sasha stayed mid-ship, one hand settled on the helm and her musings drifting like feathers in the breeze. Occasionally, she'd look out over the ocean through a spyglass Toddy had found belowdecks and given to her. It was so strange to be away from the island, far from the sparkling tents and the friendly, colorful faces at the Cirque, and far from the dull, square buildings of the school and all the taunts there.

"Where are we going?" Toddy asked one day. He sat on the steps behind Sasha, whittling a block of wood with a knife he'd discovered in the captain's quarters;

the cutlass and sheath he'd also found there was tied securely around his waist. He paused to take a bite of crackers and dried beef, which he had found in a barrel. Pirate chased the cracker crumbs that fell and blew all around the deck.

"I don't know," Sasha replied. Then added absently, "Careful, Toddy. Don't cut yourself."

"I won't. Do you think we'll find sharks? Or mermaids?"

"Mermaids would be lovely." Sasha rubbed gently at the scabs that had formed on her knees. Madame Mermadia was back at the Cirque. Was she all right? And Shelby and Griffin, too? "Or a princess."

"Do you think Mr. Ticklefar knew the seed would grow a ship? Do you think we should have taken him along with us?"

"I don't know."

"Mom probably misses us, don't you think?"

"I don't know. I hope so."

"Do you think she's lonely without us?"

"Toddy! Stop asking so many questions!" Toddy was always doing that at home. Asking Sasha very serious, important things, but also silly things. *You're the only one who really listens,* he always told her. *You and Mom and Dad, but . . . Mom and Dad listen like grown-ups. You know what I mean. You listen with . . . real imagination.*

"I would ask Pirate, but he never met Mom and Dad."

"Maybe you should ask Pirate where we're going."

Toddy shook his head. "I did already. He doesn't know. But he's keeping his claws sharp, just in case."

Toddy returned to the helm. He scaled the ropes like a mouse. How far could he see, up there? Sasha followed him up, picking her way carefully into the sky.

Once she'd reached the top and Toddy had helped her into the basket, Sasha walked in a circle to take in the scenery. A line of creamy Orangesicle sunset stretched as far as she could see to the south. To the north the sea was interrupted by dots of dancing gray seals and long brown shorelines.

It reminded her of Anders' Rock on the island, where she and Toddy and Mom and Dad would picnic on days bursting with warmth. There they would search out turquoise sea glass and glittering silver rocks spit from volcanoes millions of years ago. Dad drilled tiny holes into them, and Mom strung them on twine to wear around their necks. *We all belong to the land and the sea,* she'd say, and they'd all get quiet and watch the waves lick the shore. Until Toddy got bored, and then they'd hop into the water and splash one another until they were shivering and desperate to climb back onto the rock to sun themselves toasty warm again, waiting for a colorful sunset to drop onto the island.

"Magic. I think we're almost to the Edge of the World," she said, pointing to the masses of seals. She squinted as the sun glinted off the dots.

As if to confirm her comment, the ship gave a mighty roar and teetered to the left. The masts whipped around them like tree branches in a thunderstorm. Sasha and Toddy grasped onto the basket with white knuckles and startled gasps. On the deck Pirate screeched.

Below them the sea churned, crashing this way and that, a whirlpool spinning just off starboard. Slowly a creature rose from the foaming white depths.

Sasha and Toddy gaped at the monster. Knobby green legs as long as a highway, topped with purple claws as big as a school bus, lifted into the air, breaking the agitated surface of the water with a wretched, piercing noise and a waterfall of ocean. Waving white tentacles reached to the clouds, and two eyes, like black boulders at the shore, narrowed as the creature spotted Sasha and Toddy in the crow's nest. The creature's mouth worked slowly, its fangs dripping salt water back into the sea.

"Who trespasses upon my ocean?"

Sharp, rotten fish-smelling winds rushed through Sasha's and Toddy's hair as the creature spoke. They took an involuntary step backward and clasped each other's hands.

"I said, who dares traverse my sea?"

"Well, no, you didn't," Sasha said, poking her chin at the creature. "You asked who was trespassing, not who was traversing."

The creature blinked his glassy eyes at Sasha and let loose a sound that might have been laughter. It was a rumble that stirred up the ocean to choppy white peaks.

"I am King Crab, and you do not have permission to cross here."

"Are you the Magician at the Edge of the World?" Toddy asked. "You're stinky."

Time seemed to pause for Sasha. For a moment she forgot that King Crab was huge, frightening, and in their way.

"Oh!" Sasha gaped at her brother. "You're talking to someone that's not me."

"I had to tell him about his smelly breath," Toddy said.

Sasha nodded. "It's terrible."

"Besides, we both have to be braver now," Toddy said.

"Yes." Sasha snuck to the rear of the crow's nest and began descending the shrouds.

"The Magician is far beyond me," roared King Crab. "But it is impossible to pass through my sea to get to him!"

Halfway down the shrouds Sasha jutted her chin out. "Then we are in the right place. Let us through!"

"Go back to where you came from!" King Crab retorted.

Toddy brandished his sword and pointed it at the monster. "We shall never leave this sea! I demand that you let us through!"

"You must defeat me first!"

"We shall!" Toddy hollered as loudly as he could, then frowned, disappointed that the seas didn't thrash as he did so. He turned to the side. "Sasha?"

"You have been abandoned!" King Crab screeched triumphantly.

"No, I haven't." But Toddy's voice came out weaker than before, and he searched the shrouds for his sister. "Sasha?" All he saw was her retreating back, hurrying belowdecks.

King Crab laughed and whipped a claw at Toddy. With a battle cry Toddy swung his sword at the claw. The *clang!* could be heard for miles.

Sasha rushed to the gun deck. She glanced at the stalwart cannons. Hopelessness washed over her. They must have weighed hundreds of pounds. There was no way a girl a quarter of their size could maneuver and load one. Even if she knew how to load it.

She turned back to look for other ways to fight

King Crab, but paused when her eyes fell upon a diagram inked on the wall. It was a series of pictures that showed how to load the cannons. Excitement washed over Sasha, until she realized that the cannon was being handled by two full-grown men in the pictures. Full-grown and very burly.

Sasha clutched at her shirt in desperation. She was strong, she knew she was. But as strong as two men? Kirk Stoddard's words rang in her ears. *Sausage here thinks she's the toughest of us all.* Well . . . yes. Except for the *Sausage* part. Sasha pursed her lips. Her eyes flashed with determination. The cannon beckoned to her, and she had to try. She would show everyone how tough she was. She reached out her hands, gripped the base of the gun, and pulled.

"Oh!"

Sasha fell backward, flat onto her behind, as the gun slid smoothly out of its port. She blinked but stood quickly and consulted the diagram. "Rope . . . goes in this way and . . . out here. Then . . . sand?"

Sasha winced at the sounds of battle above her. "*Hurry*, Sasha," she told herself.

She peered into the dark shadows of the deck. The sack in the corner looked promising. She pulled the top back and dipped her hands into the black grains, wrinkling her nose at the acrid smell. "Drop this down this part and shove . . . paper? Paper." Sasha looked around again but found only disorderly piles of old, torn sail. "This will have to work."

Sasha collected a length of the sail and pushed it into the cannon with the rammer, her arms aching with the effort. "Time for the cannonball."

The cannonball was a glass marble, swirling milk and honey, and it whispered terms of courage to Sasha and emboldened her so that she could do what she needed to do. Sasha took it into her hands; it was as big as a bowling ball and heavy. It clanged like the first strike of a gong when Sasha dropped it into the barrel. She shoved the rammer in once more, for good measure, and braced the balls of her feet against the slippery wooden floor. The cannon turned toward the port. Outside, King Crab's legs scraped and flailed as the creature tried to get a grip on the ship's planks. Pirate leaped gracefully all over the monster, swatting and biting at the tender joints in between King Crab's armor.

"Mrowr!" Pirate declared as he landed a particularly good chomp.

"Avast, ye, enemy!" Toddy cried. There was a vicious clang of metal against shell and more wordless shouts.

Sasha's heart pounded painfully. "Please be all right, Toddy."

She was all he had left. And he . . . was all she had too.

The last scene in the diagram on the wall showed a

crewman dashing two objects together to create a spark for lighting the fuse. Sasha stared at the picture for several seconds, her stomach clenching.

"After all this, I don't know how to make a fire."

Her hand dropped to her side. Her fingers fell upon her spyglass, tapped along the worn leather sides in frustration, and smoothed over the cool glass magnifier. Sasha started.

With a swoop of her hand she lifted the spyglass from her belt and examined the brass instrument. The large glass piece at the end was attached to a ring. Sasha fit her palm around the ring and twisted. It was rather tight, but after a few seconds of work, she loosened the ring, and the glass piece fell into her hand. There was just enough room above the cannon to catch a beam of fading sunlight. Sasha held the glass between the beam and the fuse.

"Keep steady, hand," Sasha whispered. Everything—the ship, the sea—seemed to wait silently for the fuse to catch. And when it did, and Sasha had blown on it gently until it sizzled like bacon in a frying pan, the world came alive again.

"Your defeat is nigh!" Toddy bellowed to King Crab. Despite the raging battle, Sasha had to hold back a giggle. He sounded just like Mr. Ticklefar back at the Cirque when the old ringmaster introduced an act, saying, *Danger is nigh!*

The ship groaned and creaked as it tossed. Water splashed against the exterior with a roar like an African lion. Pirate yowled.

King Crab snapped his claws with a triumphant *clack!* Sasha peered out the hole and shrieked: Toddy was clamped in one of King Crab's claws. A flash of color whizzed across Sasha's line of vision. A bird . . . one she'd seen before. It attacked one of King Crab's eyes. The great beast waved his claws in the air.

"Toddy!" The fuse went silent. The whole world did, just for a moment.

Then . . . *BOOM!* The entire deck shook. Sasha fell flat onto the floor while water rose in waves all around her. Millions of particles hit the ship and splashed in the water. Sasha's body rolled and swayed with the motion of the sea. When the quaking ceased, all was quiet. The only sound was a low buzzing in Sasha's ears.

"Toddy?" Sasha said, even though Toddy couldn't possibly hear her from the gun deck. Sasha couldn't even hear herself. She raced to the top deck and leaned over the railing, searching the seas for her brother and Pirate the cat. First Dad and then Mom. She didn't know what she would do if she lost Toddy. "Toddy!"

The sea took on a horrible stillness, the water like mirror-glass. Sasha looked left and right, searching desperately for some sign of her brother. The tears that welled up in her eyes made her vision blurry, but she angrily wiped them clean. She had lost her whole family. It was all her fault they were gone.

Sasha's heart squeezed and squished until she couldn't breathe. She would do anything—anything!—to get her family back again. How could she have ever wanted anything but to be with Mom and Dad and Toddy at Cirque Magnifique?

Just then a bit of seashell bounced off Sasha's head. No, not seashell but crab shell. Sasha looked up. Dangling over the rail of the crow's nest by his legs was a boy with a kitten clinging to the front of his shirt. He waved both his arms at her, mouthed something, and pulled himself back into the basket. Sasha jumped to her feet and raced across the deck. At the same time, Toddy descended by sliding down the mast. He looked a bit worse for the battle, with a long scratch along one cheek and his clothes in tatters. When they met in the middle, Sasha flung her arms around her brother, squashing poor Pirate, and cried even harder.

"That ol' beast!" Toddy yelled. "He couldn't keep me in his big claws. Not after you blew him to smithereens! He flung me into the air. It was a good thing I landed on the ship. I was yelling at you for ages, though. Why didn't you look up?"

Sasha shook her head with confusion. King Crab

had let go of Toddy, but not because of the blast. Because of . . .

Had she really seen the bird, or had she only imagined it? She couldn't think properly. The buzzing in her ears was too loud. "It doesn't matter. You're here! And we're going to find that horrid Magician and get Mom and Dad back."

They stood together to look over the side of the ship. King Crab floated upon the sea in dozens of pieces.

"Ew," Sasha wrinkled her nose.

"Don't worry, the gulls will take care of it. See?" Toddy pointed to the horizon, where a swarm of sleek white birds were racing to the scene. Sasha and Toddy watched as the first of the birds landed upon the sea and began to feast. One even turned to them and nodded its appreciation.

Sasha squinted, looking for color in the sea of white. But there was none.

"They'll always remember you for this," Toddy said. "You're the queen of the seas now, Sasha. That was a super shot. How'd you do it?"

Sasha clutched her brother to her. Relief overwhelmed her. "There was a diagram . . . and we have to be braver now, and . . . I'm just glad we're past King Crab."

Toddy nodded. "Now let's get Mom and Dad."

CHAPTER 21

When Sasha slept that night, she dreamed that thousands of tropical birds circled the ship, nudging it in the direction Sasha wanted to go. In the morning Sasha rubbed sleep from her eyes and pressed her palms over her ears, glad to have all her hearing back. There were no birds around the ship, but there was something else.

When she climbed to the very front of the forecastle, Sasha let out a soft breath. It was dashed away on the wind. She squinted. "Land." Down on deck Toddy scrubbed the brass knobs and sang pirate songs. "Toddy, land!"

The song ended abruptly as Toddy raced to join Sasha. They watched, frozen and silent, the small, dark lump of land come closer and closer. A shrill, cold wind blew over their arms. Ice floes bumped into the sides of the ship, gently rocking the boat from side to side.

The sky was turning a strange shade of orange-brown as the ship pushed against the sandy bottom with a *shush.* They were still too far from the land to swim, even if the sea had been balmy and blue instead of chilly and gray, so Sasha and Toddy carefully lowered into the water one of the rowboats hanging on the side of the ship and hopped in. Pirate leaped in behind them.

"Is this the Edge of the World?" Sasha said.

Pirate cocked his kitten head to the side.

It very well might have been the Edge of the World. The closer they rowed to land, the lonelier they felt. The winds picked up, brushing by them with hints of dark whispers. But on land they could see no movement. Only a long, gray beach and deep darkness beyond. Sasha pressed on her chest, trying to push away the heavy settling of fear that made her want to turn the rowboat around and go back to the Cirque.

Except that would mean never being with Mom and Dad again.

Pirate licked her hand with his warm sandpaper tongue, and that helped a little.

They rowed on until their arm muscles ached and their bellies shivered with cold.

When they reached the shore, they pulled the boat high onto the beach and faced the darkness spread out before them. There were rocks and trees, although the trees seemed spindly, with hundreds of fingers and arms pointing in all directions, and on those arms and fingers, tiny little spikes. They didn't share the space. No canopy of leafy green, no understory of tall ferns or rambling blackberry canes. But the thing Sasha and Toddy noticed most of all was that there was silence. No wind, there on land. No animal sounds or laughter or bumps or anything. And yet there was a prickle of familiarity on the back of Sasha's neck. Mr. Ticklefar had told tales of places this barren.

"I'm scared," Toddy whispered. When he spoke, it sounded like fireworks. The land seemed to soak his words into the ground and shoot them up into the sky.

Pirate scampered behind Toddy's pant leg, hissing quietly at the trees.

"Me too," Sasha said. She took her brother's hand. "But I think we're on the right track. Come on."

They moved inland slowly and carefully. Pirate picked at the land gingerly with his paws and kept his ears flat against his head. There was no trail, so they zigzagged here and there, hoping they were moving in the right direction. The right direction for what, they didn't know. Sasha only felt sure that they had to keep moving, had to delve deeper into the Forest of Thorny Trees until they reached the true Edge of the World.

When a branch fell slowly across their path, Sasha stepped forward quickly to brush it aside, wincing at the little tears in her arms and the scratches that ran across her legs like angry, red frowns.

"I'm hungry," Toddy said after they'd walked awhile.

"Me too. We should have brought food from the ship." Sasha looked behind them, wondering if they should go back, but the forest drew itself around them so thickly that they couldn't see the shore anymore. "But it's too late now. I don't know if we could even find our way back through the darkness."

So they walked on. Mist began to curl around their ankles. Sasha's chest ached again. She wanted to cry. The last time she had felt this awful was when she'd watched her parents flutter away. Suddenly she realized that the mist at her feet wasn't mist; it was the Smoke.

Of course everything felt bad. The closer she got to the Magician, the worse she would feel. He was the source of her sorrow.

"We have to hurry," Sasha told Toddy. They ran through the forest. Thorns whipped at Sasha's face and tangled her hair, making the strands stick to her teary cheeks. The Smoke rolled in more and more thickly until finally Sasha and Toddy tripped on something and fell to the ground.

They lay, covered in Smoke, trying to catch their breaths. Sasha was sure this was the end of her adventures. They would fade, slowly, into the Smoke until they ceased to exist. She had failed.

"I'm sorry, Toddy." Sasha reached a hand out to him, but he was gone. "Toddy?"

Sasha sat up, squinting through the Smoke; then she stood. A circle of Smoke cleared away, and in the center was a strange creature. Something like a weasel, but with a long, sharp beak on one end and a slinking tail on the other. A tail that at the moment was wrapped snugly around Toddy and Pirate, who was stuffed down Toddy's shirt.

"Let them go!" Sasha said.

The Sharp-Beaked Weasel spoke, his syllables long and hushed. "Food is diiifficult to find in these parts. I can't pooossibly let go of my newest catch."

"You must let him go! I need my brother," Sasha shouted. "I'll fight you. . . . I'll hurt you!"

The Sharp-Beaked Weasel picked a bit of old food from his gleaming teeth with a razor-sharp claw.

"Neeeed him? Oh, nooo. I watched the way you maaarched around here like you own this whole forest. You don't need aaanyone."

"That's not true."

"Suuuch a shame." The Weasel sniffed through his long beak. "I'm afraid you've no hope of hurting meee, girl. Good day."

The Weasel was a slow mover, turning delicately into the forest as though he, too, hated those thorny branches. Sasha moved quickly, snapping a low branch from the nearest tree and waving it like a sword.

"You'd better stop!" She swung the branch at the flanks of the Weasel. The animal yowled, and almost immediately a patch of yellow boils grew on his skin where Sasha had hit him.

"Don't dooo that, girl!" the Weasel said.

"I will. I will do it a hundred billion times until you give me my brother back."

The Weasel bared his teeth and hissed, and he looked like he could snap her in half with one chomp, but Sasha stood her ground.

The Weasel tried to scurry away, but he was much too slow, twisting and turning to avoid touching the spiny trees. She saw the boils on the Weasel's side, and it dawned on her: the trees were some kind of poison to him. She swept the branch at the Weasel again, this time catching one of the creature's rear paws.

The Weasel whimpered. Sweat glistened on his brow. "Stooop that!"

Sasha hesitated. She had a weapon and could hurt the Weasel, but the animal's sharp claws could tear into Toddy, too. He didn't want to ruin his dinner, and Sasha didn't want to lose her brother. They were at an impasse.

Mr. Ticklefar's stories flashed through her mind. She had to challenge the Weasel to a riddle. He couldn't refuse. But riddles were hard. *She's stupid and doesn't even know it.* It's what the island kids always said. Sometimes Sasha worried they were right. Still . . . Sasha would figure out the Weasel's riddle even if it took her a hundred years. She was *not* stupid.

Sasha stood tall. "I challenge you to a riddle."

The Weasel narrowed his eyes. "Who told you to do that?" the Weasel growled. "All right, girl. I will giiive you a riddle. If you get it right, I let him go. If you get it wrong, he is my diiinner. The furry, squirmy thing will be dessert."

"Agreed. What is your riddle?"

The Weasel sat back on his haunches, Toddy still wrapped neatly in his tail.

"There once was a sister and a brother. We shall call them Giiirl and Diiinner. They each had a rowboat that they claimed was the fastest rowboat eeever created. Girl's was blue and Dinner's was yellow. They fought and argued, as brothers and sisters always do, for who hates each other more than faaamily?" The Weasel's gaze fell on Sasha, as if he knew all her secrets. Sasha shrank back with shame. She wished the Weasel had her instead of Toddy.

"Ooone day," the Weasel continued, "they came

upon a Magician. 'I will solve the dilemma of the fastest rowboat,' the Magician said. 'Do you seeee that island? Row to it, then row back to me. If Girl's boat gets here first, Girl wins. If Dinner's boat reaches me first, then Dinner wins. The loooser drowns, never to be seen again. Reeeady, go!' So they rowed to the island. When they got there, they were tired. They got out and rested. When they were done resting, Girl tossed one set of oars into the water, grabbed the other, and rowed as faaast as she could to the Magician. Then she drowned and was never seen again. Hooow did she lose?"

How strange, Sasha thought, that the faster rower would be the loser, instead of the winner. It didn't make sense. The Magician said the one who didn't make it back first would drown. But some sense *had* to be made of it. If she couldn't figure the riddle out, she would lose Toddy and Pirate. And she'd do anything not to lose all she had left of her family.

Sasha would have liked to sit on the ground to think. There was something about sitting that made her brain work better. But the Smoke still wrapped thin tendrils around the lowest parts of the forest. Instead Sasha walked.

She went in a slow circle, never letting the Sharp-Beaked Weasel or Toddy out of her sight. Her hand went to one of the thorny trees, and Sasha was surprised to find that the trunks weren't as prickly as the gnarled branches. They were as smooth as silk, coated with a shiny, dried sap that gave them that dark gray color that made the whole forest look like it had just seen a wildfire. There was something about them that almost glistened, as though if only the sun shone on the forest, the trees would shine and glitter like Cirque Magnifique under the big tent. Sasha rubbed those trunks. She felt like the trees, inside. Gnarled and pokey in some places, and smooth and lustrous in others. Being a little girl was a complicated thing.

"They go to the island. . . . Girl races her boat back. . . . She wins, but she *loses*, too. How does she win and lose? Did her brother do something? No, he was resting on the island. Safe."

Sasha bit her lip, the riddle going round and round in her head as she went round and round in the forest. Her heart thumped so loudly that she could hardly think. A sheen of sweat built on her forehead. If she didn't get this right, she would lose Toddy.

She could never lose Toddy. She would never let him get eaten by the Sharp-Beaked Weasel. She would *never* let her brother die.

Just like the girl in the riddle.

And that's when she knew.

Sasha stood in front of the Weasel, her fists on her

hips, her eyes narrowed fiercely, her heart bursting, now with love. As though he knew what was coming, Pirate meowed triumphantly.

"Girl stole her brother's boat. They were on the island resting, and she took his yellow boat and rowed back to the Magician because she could never let her brother die. She loved him and wanted to take care of him. And that's the answer to the riddle!"

The Weasel made a terrible sound, like the screeching of a hundred seabirds, and fell over onto his back. He writhed and wiggled and threw the biggest tantrum Sasha had ever seen. But she didn't care, because his tail also loosened and Toddy came tumbling out.

Sasha ran to him and gathered him in her arms. The little group of three ran farther into the forest without a backward glance at the Weasel.

CHAPTER 22

They walked and walked. It was possible they walked for days. Maybe for years. All the trees blended together until Sasha felt certain she didn't know anything, not the shape of a circle or the taste of soup. All she knew was the never-ending weight of exhaustion.

She pushed one foot in front of the other, moving along automatically. Slowly the sky changed from a sullen gray to a pale, milky blue. Ahead of them a trail climbed into the sky along the perimeter of a shadowy hillside. Thick evergreens swathed the hill in shadows, and ferns grew underfoot in hundreds of hues of green. Pirate darted in and out of them, chasing bugs.

"Should we see where the trail goes?" Sasha asked, as though she and Toddy had any choice but to follow.

"Maybe that way will finally take us to the Edge of the World."

"I don't want to walk that far. I don't want to walk at all anymore."

"Well, we can't go back the way we came," Sasha said, sharper than she'd meant to. She took Toddy's hand again. She was only tired and hungry. "And I bet we'll find Mom and Dad up there."

Toddy gave a skeptical sound but said: "All right."

They walked for a while longer, Sasha keeping the pace slow so that Toddy's tiredness and hunger wouldn't bother him so much. She told a story about a magic train that traveled on golden tracks, carrying jewels and toys. The train fell from the sky and, when all the jewels and toys were delivered, dug itself into the very earth to hibernate the winter away.

When the ground beside the trail began to drop off sharply on one side, and the rock and foliage of the trees crept in on the other, she began to sing a song about elephants, softly at first, but then louder as they climbed up and up the hill. She turned her face to the sky to catch the rest of the late afternoon's rays, and Toddy followed along until they were both grinning at a lemon gumdrop sun surrounded by cotton ball clouds.

Sasha and Toddy were so busy singing that they forgot about the distance. They walked on, at times lifting their knees high in a marching step like soldiers and other times dragging their shoes through loose pebbles and fern roots. Bits of grit and hard nuggets tumbled through the holes in their soles, and after a while they had to sit and take their shoes off, to shake the matter out.

"You all right?" Toddy asked Pirate. "Keeping your strength up eating bugs? Good."

Sasha wrinkled her nose. Then they were off again, holding hands and climbing higher and higher up the side of the hill. The air was cooler and thinner up there, so that little goose bumps sprang up on their bare arms. Toddy slowed to a stop and dropped Sasha's hand. He sniffed and rubbed his nose with the hem of his shirt.

"I'm tired, Sasha. When are we going to get there?"

Sasha pulled herself out of her singsong daydream and looked about, surprised to find that the sun was falling out of their world and into another one. The tree shadows were long enough to cover them like a blanket. Sasha's belly rumbled.

"Let's sit down for a second and clean out our shoes again," Sasha said. She needed time to think.

They sat on a fallen log, wincing as wood pressed into the backs of their tired legs. Sasha pulled off her shoes and shook them out, gazing around under her lashes.

They only needed to retrace their steps back the way they had come to get home. But that would mean traversing the Forest of Thorny Trees and rowing out to the pirate ship and crossing all those seas again. Toddy looked miserable sitting next to her, and it was such a long way . . . to home or to the Edge of the World. He licked his lips hungrily and sighed. His legs weren't as long as Sasha's, which must have meant they were twice as tired. She couldn't make him walk all the way back without having something to eat first.

Sasha had truly believed that they would find the Magician up that hill. It was impossible to think that no one lived in the woods or that there wasn't a snug fairy-tale cabin full of singing woodland critters nestled among the trees on the hill. *She* would live there, if given the chance.

And wasn't it funny that even though they had climbed very high, she still could not look down and see the seas? All the Smoke blocked everything below, and the green blocked everything above. Life seemed full and thick here, and also lonely. They hadn't seen another Sharp-Beaked Weasel. Was the one that had given her the riddle the only one in existence?

But they were not alone. Sasha was sure Toddy didn't hear the first shrieking caw, because he didn't move an inch as it sounded. But when he turned his wide eyes to

Sasha after a few seconds' quiet pause led into a second fierce shriek, she wrapped her arm around his shoulders and pulled him tight to her side. Pirate hid under their knees, his eyes glowing through the gap.

"What was that?" Toddy whispered.

Sasha gazed into the trees, into a darkness that grew as the gumdrop sun melted into the horizon. A branch rattled two trees away from them. Sasha squinted at the tree and around it. There was no more movement. It must have been a short burst of wind; the breeze chilled her bare legs.

The animal screamed again, and Sasha changed her mind. It certainly wasn't the angry wind crying out but something that set her heart racing. Sasha bit back her fear and scanned the treetops, searching for the creature.

"There," she said, relieved, pointing. "Do you see him? He's probably just finished his dinner. Or maybe he's letting all the other birds know we're here."

They watched the black-and-white sea eagle behind the branches plunge his hooked raptor beak under an outstretched wing and tidy the feathers. He gave a puffed shake, then stilled, focusing his dark, round eyes as though he were waiting for Sasha and Toddy to pick up their end of the conversation. He cocked his head at them. Sasha cocked hers back, an odd sense of recognition filling her belly.

Before she could decide what was so familiar, the sea eagle's eyes shot to the ground. He opened his eight-foot wingspan briefly to raise himself off the branch, then closed his wings in and dove for the earth. He rushed down like a flash of light and rose again from the forest floor like a phoenix, clutching his dinner in his mighty talons and shooting into the darkness of the thick forest.

The world went silent.

Sasha waited, but the sea eagle didn't return. Her eyes drooped.

Dusk sounds picked up around them; rasping frogs, calling night birds, and chirruping crickets dulled their senses until Toddy's head slumped against her side in the heavy weight of sleep. Pirate curled up into a ball in Toddy's lap and let loose a huge yawn. Sasha rested her head atop Toddy's and breathed deeply of the damp, earthy air around them.

CHAPTER 23

Sasha awoke with a jerk. There was something strange in the air. Something that chilled her spine and prickled her instincts. The world swayed as though it wanted to rock her back to sleep, but she remained frozen and awake.

The trees were quiet. All the sounds of evening that had lulled them to sleep were gone. The green branches had turned tar black in the night, and she didn't want to look at them, for fear she would be lost in them. The world was so big; would anyone remember they once existed in their small town if the darkness ended up swallowing them whole?

The only noise was her breath, and Toddy's slow, rhythmic breathing that indicated he was asleep. And . . . and . . .

a *crunch.* A shuffling of pine needles, then another *crunch.* Again and again, and then . . . a rocking motion! They were moving! Sasha's eyes went as wide as dinner plates, and all remnants of sleep dashed away. A pungent smell reached her nose, and her hands dug into something warm, with crispy hairs.

That was not the ground.

"Toddy," she whispered. "Pirate. Wake up." She nudged her brother gently. "Wake up."

His eyes fluttered. He wiped the back of his hand across his mouth. Pirate stirred, looked at them disdainfully with one eye, and went back to sleep. "What?" Toddy asked.

"I think . . . there's an animal. Beneath us."

"Is it the sea eagle again?"

"No. Feel it? Something that walks on the ground."

"Is it a turtle?"

It could have been, with how steadily it moved. But there was the hair. And the smell. "I don't think so."

A low voice tumbled through the air to Sasha and Toddy. "Is that you critters awake up there?"

The brother and sister shared a wide-eyed look. Sasha cleared her throat and searched for a bit of bravery beneath the fear that blanketed her skin.

"Yes. Who . . . what are you?"

The rocking motion stopped, and Sasha felt the

bottom drop out of her stomach as they were quickly lowered to the ground. She gripped the thing's hair more tightly, working hard not to topple over. When the creature was still again, she slid to the ground and slowly tiptoed around to what she assumed was the front of the creature.

It was at least as big as the horses from Cirque Magnifique. Thicker, though, and possibly taller, with legs that seemed too skinny for how big its humped body and head were. And that head . . . it was nothing short of majestic, with a long, fat nose; dark, oval eyes; and massive antlers jutting from the sides of its head.

But the most interesting and beautiful part of the animal was the glistening silver line running up the creature's nose right to a spot between the antlers, where a glittering rainbow horn perched. Sasha's brain searched through the wild and wonderful tales of strange creatures Mr. Ticklefar had told her, but she couldn't recall hearing about an animal like this one. So she made up her own name.

"Are you a . . . Unimoose?"

The huge animal bowed its head and front legs to Sasha far more gracefully than she would have expected from an animal its size.

"Unfortunately, I am not a Unimoose. I am *the* Unimoose. The last of my kind." The Unimoose gave a gentle hum. It was a sad, searching sound. "There used to be a few more of us. We'd come to this forest at this time of year to eat the trundleberries. They are so delicate and delicious. Most of the large animals that roam these parts lack the gentleness required to pick them, but Unimoose have a special way of separating the leaves with our racks and licking the berries from the stem. We'd compete to see who could find the most and decorate that Unimoose with a crown woven from the branches of the stardust trees at the Edge of the World."

"The Edge of the World! You know the place?"

"Yes, of course. We all do, but we stay here. Closer to safety. Even the Leaping Scorch Bat and Low-Lying Soil Ray avoid *that* place. It is only the Round-Tailed Preying Cats that dare venture there. Well, they venture everywhere. In fact, that's why I picked you two up when I saw you sleeping on the ground. I've never seen your species before, and it may be that you have hidden defenses, but your teeth and your claws and your size and your strength, well, don't seem the best match for the cats. And *your* little cat . . . it's smaller than a Preying Cat newborn, you see. Pardon me for saying."

"Not at all. We don't want to be a meal for the Preying Cats. Thank you for not leaving us to get eaten."

"My pleasure. However, I don't quite know where

it is you came from or where it is you want to go, so I've just been walking in circles all night."

Sasha's tummy rumbled. She inspected her fingers. The nails were filthy, but they certainly weren't claws. That was probably a good thing, for what she was about to say.

"We do have a place to be, but first . . ." Her tummy gurgled again and her words rushed out. "If you don't mind, we would like to challenge you to a trundleberry-picking competition! That is, we don't have a garland for the winner, we don't know what trundleberries look like, and we don't know how to pick them, but if you would be so kind as to show us, we could pretend we were your old Unimoose friends."

The Unimoose's line of silver sparkled, and its horn glowed brightly. "I love that idea! Challenge accepted."

"And after, would you take us to the Edge of the World?"

The Unimoose blinked its long lashes and put its face close enough to Sasha that she could feel its breath on her face.

"No. I cannot. I will not go there, and you must not. It's too dangerous. It's where all the other Unimoose were lost." The Unimoose shook its head. "A terrible, awful place. You may stay with me as long as you like, though. I rather enjoy carrying you around, and you have a nice voice. I'm guessing you can sing or tell stories."

"Only just for fun. But please. We really, truly must get to the Edge of the World. Our parents need us to do this." Sasha's voice dipped to a mouse-like whisper. "I need to do this."

The Unimoose gave its low hum again, a sound that made the whole world seem a little sadder. It watched Sasha for a long time, perhaps seeing something in her that even Sasha herself couldn't see. Finally the Unimoose lowered its head in a sign of acceptance.

"I can't take you all the way, but I can take you as far as the Grandelion."

"The Grandelion?" Toddy asked.

"The gatekeeper to the garden at the Edge of the World. A huge, terrible creature. Fierce and bitter. The Grandelion will not let you past . . . but alas, I cannot stop you from trying."

CHAPTER 24

Sasha scrambled onto the Unimoose's back again and, as the sun rose over the horizon, they moved deeper into the shrubs. She loved the rolling gait of the Unimoose's long legs beneath her. Her body relaxed, and soon she was remembering the times when the Cirque Magnifique horse masters let her ride with them during training. During shows the horses, too, would be decked out in silver and rainbows, but their slow walks changed when the lights hit them. They became energized, soaking in the attention from the audience, prancing proudly with their colorful riders on their backs, or holding steady as their riders did marvelous tricks like handstands in the saddle or leaps from horse to horse.

"We're here," the Unimoose said. "Look for bright

orange berries, not green ones. They're ready when they're swollen with juice and sweetly fragrant."

On either side of the trail, canes twisted up toward the sky. They were covered in tiny thorns and round, neon-orange berries with five-sided tops like star-shaped hats. There was one ripe berry almost within reach of Sasha, so she put her hand out and stretched her whole body, sliding slightly off the Unimoose, to get it.

"Ouch!" She snatched her arm away, sticking her sore fingertips into her mouth. Those thorns were prickly!

"That's what most of the creatures hereabout say," the Unimoose said. "My kind have special, thick tongues to protect us from the thorns, but you—"

"Have quickness and small size," Toddy said.

"Yeah!" Sasha agreed. "Come on, Toddy. We just have to find all the little spaces and openings between the canes. It'll be like playing hide-and-seek from Mr. Ticklefar back at the Cirque. Ready, go!"

The Unimoose lowered itself so that Sasha and Toddy and Pirate could slide to the ground, then raised its head into the sky and let loose a mighty bellow. "To the berries!"

The group split up. The crunching sound from the Unimoose's large body in the plants nearly drowned out the shrieks and giggles from the children as they pulled vibrantly orange berries from the canes, popped them into their mouths, and shouted their count.

"Sixteen!" Sasha hollered. Flavors zinged through her mouth: the sweet tartness of the berries, the crisp freshness of the air, the salty sweat from her lips as the sun and movement heated their bodies. Sasha was sure she could battle a thousand magicians, with the joy that was racing through her.

"Fifty!" the Unimoose called out.

"Fifty?" Sasha and Toddy echoed. They looked at each other with wide eyes. Their faces were smeared with trundleberry juice, and their arms were lined with squiggly pink scratches from the thorns. Even Pirate was dotted orange in between his gray stripes.

But they burst into laughter as though they had forgotten about all their cares—their missing parents, the fearsome Grandelion, the even more terrible Magician—and dove back into berry picking.

When their bellies were full to bursting and their fingers swollen with pricks, Sasha and Toddy found a small clearing and fell to the ground. The Unimoose joined them, and all four savored the cool grass beneath them.

"That was magic," Sasha said.

The Unimoose snorted. "Magic is all well and good, but that was nothing more than hard work. It's important to understand the difference."

"Don't you believe in magic?"

"Of course I do, but there has to be a balance between

the things that the universe controls and the things that we control. Are you a puppet on a string, little critter?"

At Cirque Magnifique there were dancing horses, twirling-ribbon acrobats, flying-trapeze artists, contortionists who could turn their bodies into pretzels. Strong men and women who could balance another three or four people on their bodies. Imaginarionists who built otherworldly sets and decorated them with bits and baubles, glitter and glitz.

There were children of entertainers, who learned their parents' arts, who helped every day with mundane tasks like sweeping the tents and clearing away weeds, and who marveled at the shining beauty of it all. And there was Mr. Ticklefar, who bossed everyone around to make sure the Cirque was truly magnificent.

But there were no puppets.

Sasha shook her head and stood. "We have to go. I must find the Magician, because you're right, dear Unimoose, I can't leave my destiny up to the universe. I must create it myself."

The Unimoose got to its feet slowly and blinked its long eyelashes sadly. "If I controlled the universe, I would find happiness for you in your world, little critter. But this journey is yours to control, and now I must take you to the Grandelion."

CHAPTER 25

The sun beat down, making things hotter and hotter as the Unimoose sauntered up the trail. Soon enough the incline abated and they were walking through a strange landscape of steaming rainbow pools against a backdrop of chalk-white caves in the distance. The air smelled like rotten eggs, and Sasha and Toddy covered their faces with their shirts.

"Always stay on the path when going through the Rainbow Valley," the Unimoose cautioned. "It's many a creature that has fallen into those pools and never been seen again."

Sasha leaned over as far as she dared to peer into the sapphire depths of one pool, but the water went on forever and she couldn't see the bottom.

"What happens to the creatures?" Toddy asked.

"I don't rightly know. They go in, but they're never able to come out. I suppose it's the heat. Or perhaps that strange smell means there's something deadly in the pools."

"They're so beautiful," Sasha whispered. She leaned even more, keeping her palms wrapped tightly in the Unimoose's fur. But part of her wanted to let go. To drop into those mystical depths and envelop herself in the millions of colors. How nice it would be to forget about all her cares and all the tasks ahead of her.

The Unimoose harrumphed and bucked so that Sasha bounced in the air and landed solidly in the middle of its back again. "Now *that's* a strange magic, in those pools. They don't care that any creature wants to make their own destiny. They'll lure you in all the same."

"I'd really love to . . . just a finger, maybe . . . ," Sasha said.

"No!" Toddy grabbed his sister around the waist and held her tight. Even Pirate sank his teeth into Sasha's shirt and wouldn't let go. "We have to get to the Magician. We have to get Mom and Dad back."

A fog lifted from Sasha's mind, and she cleared her throat. "It's like they're talking to me," she said. "They want me to come in. I don't like it."

"The closer you get to the Edge of the World, the

harder everything around you works to keep you away. It's not a nice place."

"Then why do you stay so near the Edge of the World? Since *you're* so nice," Sasha said.

"It's my home. And sometimes it becomes our duty to stay in our homes and make them the lovely places we want them to be. Ah." The Unimoose stopped. "The Grandelion. Just ahead."

Sasha craned her neck so that she could see around the Unimoose's grand antlers and rainbow horn. Ahead, the rainbow pools were obscured by a tall stone tunnel, pale gray on the outside, where the sun shone merrily, but deepest dark inside, where shadows crept and crawled like long-limbed rats.

"I don't want to go in there," Toddy said.

"I don't either." Sasha rubbed her arms even though it was very warm out.

The Unimoose grinned. "I'll gladly take you three back to the trundleberry patches. Let's go."

"No, friend." Sasha dismounted, took the Unimoose's nose in her hands and pressed her forehead against the sleek silver line there. Comfort filled her chest, and her bravery was renewed. "I know you'd rather keep us away from this place, but we have to go. Our parents, our home . . . they're counting on us. Even if they don't know it."

"A brave thing to say. And a braver thing to do. Take care, then, little critters." The Unimoose turned away, retracing their steps back through the Rainbow Valley, and disappeared into the thick mists and swirls of Smoke.

CHAPTER 26

Sasha swept Pirate up on her shoulder and stepped into the tunnel. She kept her brother tucked behind her, with hands on his wrists and her eyes on the walls. They moved, those walls. She was certain of it. Black squiggles against more black, so she shouldn't have been able to see anything strange, but the hairs on her arms stood as tall as trees, and she kept looking left and right as though following *something.*

It was cold in the tunnel. And damp. The eggy smell of the valley got stuck in there, transforming into something moldy and ancient. Every time Sasha took a breath in, it felt like the tunnel took a breath as well. And when she let her breath out, her clothes brushed against her body in the slight breeze. Something itched the back of Sasha's neck. She reached her hand around to scratch it, and discovered that her neck was fuzzy and velvety and that her fingers sank into depths of softness.

She bit back a scream and pushed Toddy ahead of her. "Run," she said.

The sounds of their movements echoed in the tunnel, caught by the shadows and tossed toward them again with a new lushness until their ears felt full of cotton. Every step Sasha took brought on a new impulse to break out into sobs, but she would not give in. For, as terrifying as moving through the shadows was, it was even more frightening to think about stopping to cry. Letting those nefarious shadows gather around her and stroke her hair and skin, enter her being through her nose and mouth. Take her over.

So she and Toddy ran until they were out of breath, and then they ran some more. The trundleberries, so sweet and delicious before, now sloshed around in their stomachs with a bitterness that made Sasha ill. She was never going to get through the tunnel. She was never going to find the Magician. And she certainly was never going to defeat the Smoke. How absurd to think a child was capable of anything like that!

"Agh!" Toddy tripped over an uneven stone and rolled to the ground. Sasha tumbled over him, twisting and turning like she was barreling down a hill. Her elbow slammed into the ground painfully, and dirt collected in her hair.

This was the end, she thought. But she kept her body rolling, like the Cirque Magnifique contortionists who gathered themselves tightly and spun themselves around the big tent like pill bugs, their sequins flashing in the lights until the audience was too dazzled to understand what was real and what was fantasy.

Sasha's dizziness was so great that the shadows' dark colors spun into streaks of white. But she knew Toddy was beside her, so she kept going. Until, finally, the tunnel spit them out.

Sasha flung her limbs over the soft dirt outside the tunnel exit. The sun shone again, warming their skin and burning off any remnants of the shadows' downy clutches. Her stomach settled and her brain stopped spinning. She turned to her brother.

"Are you all right?"

Toddy's giggle was more relief than amusement, but all the same he said, "That was fun!"

Sasha got up and brushed her hands together. "Not the kind of fun I want to try again. But if we can get through the tunnel, we can survive the Grandelion. It can't be worse than—"

"Sasha!" Toddy's big eyes stared at a spot over his sister's shoulder. He scooted back a few inches and pointed.

Dread crawled up Sasha's spine like hundreds of beetles. She had a feeling she knew what was behind her, but as she slowly turned, she realized nothing could have prepared her for the greatness that was the Grandelion.

CHAPTER 27

Even before Sasha had turned around fully, she noticed that the Grandelion hummed. Vibrations unsettled the ground and rose like a buzz through her feet and up her legs.

"It's saying hello," Toddy said.

"What?" Sasha squinted at her brother.

"The Grandelion is talking. Can't you hear it? The buzzing is words."

Words . . . as though spoken by a million bumblebees all at once. Dozens of sawtooth leaves, the size of a three-story carnival slide, swayed up and down. Sometimes they swayed in a way that let Sasha peek between them and see a tall, thick stem in the distance topped with a fuzzy white ball as big as the sun.

Sasha swallowed and shook her head. "It can't talk. It's only a plant."

"Listen," Toddy said.

Sasha made a doubtful sound in the back of her throat, but did as Toddy said. To her surprise, when she cleared her mind and really listened, sound came together into words.

The buzzing quickened and rolled, like the Grandelion was laughing.

"Only a plant? A weed, *in fact!"*

The buzzing paused. Then the Grandelion laughed again, softly this time.

"An edible weed," the Grandelion added.

The laughter became too much. The ground rumbled. Cracking sounds made Sasha fear that the earth was going to open up and swallow them whole. She looked over her shoulder to see bits of stone sprinkling off the tunnel and the shadows inside swirling like brownie batter in a mixing bowl. Sasha and Toddy held tight to each other, trying to keep their balance.

The laughter slowed. It stopped. *"Have a nibble, then."*

Sasha remembered reading a book about a girl who ate things she wasn't supposed to. It got her into no end of trouble. She grew large, she shrank down. Sasha was clever enough to have learned her lesson from the girl in that book. The trundleberries were one thing; the

Unimoose was kind and it was Sasha who'd wanted to eat them. But the Grandelion was different. The way it teased Sasha and Toddy felt sinister. She was certain that if she took a bite of it, terrible things would happen.

"No, thank you," Sasha said.

"Suit yourself," the Grandelion said.

Sasha and Toddy waited, and the Grandelion leaves kept on with their waving motions, and the whole world waited for someone to make the next move.

"I challenge you to a riddle!" Sasha proclaimed.

The Grandelion hummed. "I don't play games, silly girl. I am no whimpering weasel. I am the *Grand*elion!"

Sasha pressed her lips together and narrowed her eyes. "What does the Grandelion want us to do?"

"I think—" Toddy began, but Sasha shushed him.

"I'm trying to figure this out."

"But—"

"Toddy, quiet for a minute!"

Sasha tried to look around the Grandelion, but every time she did, the big weed blocked her view with its leaves.

"I think we need to get around it," Sasha whispered. "The Edge of the World lies beyond, but it won't let us past. We don't have a cannon, like with King Crab. It didn't accept the offer of a riddle, like the Weasel. And it's not giving us a ride, like the Unimoose. I think we"—and here Sasha turned her back to the Grandelion and huddled with her brother—"should just run for it. Surprise it with our speed."

Toddy twisted his mouth. "I don't know . . ."

"It's the only way. And see, Pirate's purring. He likes the idea."

Sasha wasn't entirely convinced that Pirate liked the idea. He may have just liked how Toddy was absently stroking his back, but it didn't matter. How else could they get past the huge plant if they didn't use the element of surprise?

"One . . . two . . . go." Sasha ran straight into the thick of the Grandelion, followed closely by her brother.

Her heart raced in time with her steps, thumping against her chest and pushing the breath right out of her lungs. Panic carried her on, causing her to leap over rocks and leaves with heights she'd never achieved before, not on the journey to the Edge of the World and not at Cirque Magnifique. Until, finally, the Grandelion caught up with her.

A sawtooth leaf scooped her up like a tongue and tossed her in the air. It was like flying on the trapeze, until another leaf batted her forward and another smacked her down. Her limbs flung to and fro and her back arched painfully.

"Toddy!" she cried out, hoping her brother had

made it through, that she'd distracted the Grandelion enough to help him make his escape. But no. The next toss sent Sasha so high that she could look down and see her brother sliding down the length of a leaf, Pirate cradled in his arm.

"Sasha! Watch!" Toddy called. And that's when Sasha realized Toddy had figured out something important: the leaves were just slides. A little more complicated than a typical playground slide but toys nonetheless.

With a burst of laughter Sasha let her fear of the Grandelion dance away from her. She relaxed into the tossing up and left and right and down. Her thoughts went to all the times when she'd swung on the trapeze or scrambled down a ribbon or stood on the back of a horse. Her body—her abilities—were extraordinary, and the Grandelion was not going to take that away from her.

"My turn, Toddy!" Sasha rolled down the length of the leaf and, before she could be thrown, jumped to the next one down.

The far side of the Grandelion was in her sights. If she leaped to the right leaves, she would reach it within seconds. She jumped again and again, faster and faster as the Grandelion tried to keep up with her squirrely movements, until the buzzing grew loud and she was almost to the ground. The far side of the Grandelion was so close. Sasha paused to look over her shoulder for Toddy.

A whiplike appendage slashed her face. She fell backward, tumbled off her leaf, and landed hard on her back on the ground.

"Sasha!" Toddy tried to reach her, but the Grandelion rolled him up in a leaf and held him tight.

Sasha's breath was rattled, but she sat up slowly. "Why won't you let us pass?"

The Grandelion buzzed its laughter so hard that the world shook. Its sharp seeds stood at attention, ready to attack.

"Into the garden at the Edge of the World? Such a place of beauty the garden is. A perfect blend of colors and shapes and scents. He planted it for Lilit, you know. Brought the sun in to shine forever, and all. Left us all out here, surrounded by Smoke. Oh, how he hates your Cirque. He wants you all to suffer as he does."

"That's so . . . ," Sasha began.

"Wrong?" The Grandelion finished. All the leaves lifted, as though the Grandelion were shrugging.

Sasha pursed her lips. Yes, it was wrong to curse the Cirque. Wrong to continue to torment them. To torment her. To take her parents and to—

Sasha startled a little. It was a different thing, she suddenly realized, for the Magician to *take* her parents than it was for her to have *wished* her parents away.

And if there was a difference, whose fault was it that

her parents were gone? What had Mr. Ticklefar said to her right after her parents had been taken? *It weren't yer fault at all! 'Twas the Smoke. That dastardly devilish Magician that cursed us well before you or I was born.*

Unaware of Sasha's thoughts, the Grandelion buzzed on. *"I have so many cousins there, living a charmed life. Alas, do you know who is not allowed in the garden at the Edge of the World?"*

Sasha rubbed the back of her neck. "You. Weeds."

"Yes. I am not lovely enough. I am too encroaching. I am not wanted. And so I don't want them. *Does that sound familiar, little girl? You are not wanted anywhere either. You are like a weed, growing where you shouldn't. And everyone wants to pluck you out of existence. In turn, you refuse the help of others. Our kind don't belong in the garden. Better to accept that than to battle against it. Go back to where you came from. You are not wanted here."*

"I don't refuse help," Sasha said.

"Yes, you do, Sasha," Toddy said. "I'm good at helping take care of things. If they let me." Toddy peered at his big sister as the shadows from the Grandelion's waving leaves played across his features. "If *you* let me."

It hit Sasha that those last words were Toddy's, not the Grandelion's. She remembered something he'd said after he'd brought Pirate home. *They let me help them.*

Sasha's stomach knotted. She thought for a while.

She remembered, too, being told to stay away from a place. *You are not wanted here.* It wasn't the first time she'd heard those words. Back then only one person could cheer her up. She hung her head.

Toddy's words were true.

"Toddy . . . it wasn't just me," she said. "Getting us this far. It was barely me at all. If you hadn't been so brave . . . up there in the crow's nest on the ship. Holding King Crab captive . . . you were like Dad. High in the sky and fearless. We wouldn't be here.

"And if you hadn't given me the courage to answer the Weasel correctly, we wouldn't be here. If you hadn't helped me through Rainbow Valley and the dark tunnel and . . .

"And you know, it really began before all that. Remember when Griffin said Cirque lore wasn't true? I . . ." Sasha cast her eyes down. "I wondered sometimes if he was right. If the Smoke was just mist and Mom and Dad had . . ." But Sasha couldn't say it. After all, that was the one thing she could never believe: that her parents had simply left. "I wanted, so much, to belong somewhere new. To find some kind of middle between Cirque lore and what the Islanders said. But you never did. Mom and Dad would be proud."

Sasha's eyes filled with tears, but she didn't know why. Toddy had been a hero. Sasha hadn't expected it. Since Mom and Dad had left, she'd felt like she was the one who had to take care of him, to be his hero. But really they were a team, taking care of each other. Sasha swallowed back the tears. It was hard to admit that she couldn't do everything on her own. Pirate mewled, and that made Sasha smile. Just a tiny smile.

"You even rescued Pirate from the meanest boys at school. And remember that time when you looked at Jenny Myers and she opened the school door for us? It was like you reached her heart, somehow. You're really brave, Toddy.

"So . . ." Sasha stood. She climbed onto a low leaf and then stepped up onto another. "Toddy. Can you talk to the Grandelion? Reason with it? Reach its heart too. We just need to get past, to find the Magician. To bring our parents back to the island. I don't think anyone but you can get us past."

"Okay." Toddy climbed so high that he seemed to disappear into the white poof on top of the Grandelion. Pirate, however, darted back down to Sasha's level.

"If you're going to be a Cirque cat, you'll have to get used to heights," Sasha said.

Pirate hissed.

Toddy cleared his throat. "Hello, Grandelion. My name is Toddy. . . . Oh. You know. That's like magic. . . . Well, *I* think you're magic. I've never seen a flower so big— . . . Yes, I *do* think you are a real flower."

Toddy paused as the Grandelion buzzed mightily. He pressed his palm gently against the plant's stalk.

"I know what it's like to be different too," Toddy said. "But Miss Islip taught me that the prettiest gardens are the ones with many colors and many sizes and many smells and sounds. Maybe the Magician didn't want you in his garden, but you can make your own garden right here."

The Grandelion buzzed so softly, it was like a purr. Sasha's heart swelled for the huge plant.

Sasha slowly edged herself off the leaf and down to the next one.

Toddy continued. "Dear Grandelion, will you let us pass? The Magician tries to separate us. It's like he knows . . . if he keeps the flowers apart and . . . if he keeps people apart too, we will start to hate each other. I don't want to hate anyone."

A warm feeling spread through Sasha as she began to understand more about the Islanders. She spoke up in a trembling voice. "And I don't want anyone to hate us, either."

Sasha and Toddy and Pirate all held their breath as the Grandelion hummed. Then the hum became a buzz. The Grandelion's main stalk began to shake and the leaves swayed, and huge, fluffy seeds began to break off and float away into the vast sky. Sasha's eyes went wide, and she held on with all her might. The Grandelion shook and shook like it was filled with anger.

"Oops, no you don't." Pirate slipped off their leaf, but Sasha grabbed him by the scruff of his neck. They both dangled as the very ground rattled.

But then . . . a great wind blew as though the Grandelion were letting out a sigh. All the movement stopped. The Grandelion's seed ball drooped.

Toddy gazed at the huge plant. He nodded solemnly.

"You may pass," the Grandelion said.

Sasha grinned. "Come on, Toddy."

She gathered up Pirate, and they descended to the ground. The Grandelion leaves fell, tired, against the ground.

They ran, not knowing if the Grandelion would change its mind and scoop them off their feet again or send an army of seeds after them. Not knowing if it believed the things Toddy had said. After all, how often had her own mom and dad told her she was special, talented, smart, beautiful? And how often had Sasha chosen to believe their words?

She hadn't. But she was beginning to now.

CHAPTER 28

They ran until the sun dropped beyond the distant hills. Then they collapsed and rested. Sasha wasn't certain she had fallen asleep, but she was rattled when Toddy spoke to her. "Sasha?"

Sasha blinked, the stars above greeting her with dancing twinkles. Strangely, the Smoke was gone. Toddy stood over her, peering into her face.

"Your eyes match the sky," Sasha said.

Toddy grimaced, then extended a hand to pull her to her feet, and they looked around, their breath swirling around their faces like milky steam. Their insides were hot and their hearts beat quickly, like a downpour of rain on a roof. When the almost-dawn breeze touched their skin, they shivered.

"Where," Sasha said, gasping for the air that burned her lungs with cold, "are we now?"

"I don't know, but at least we're past the Grandelion. And look. There's a staircase."

Toddy pointed over his shoulder, where a moss-covered set of steps led from their resting spot down into the little valley.

"That must be the Edge of the World," Sasha said. "Let's go."

The two dragged their bodies through the clearing and toward the bright green trees, but when they reached the first step, they discovered that what had looked like a wall of trees wasn't one at all.

It was truly a wall.

The wall was painted just that chartreuse color that looks like morning sunbeams dappled on leaves and vines. As Sasha looked closer, she could see that there actually were dapples of cream and mint green scattered along the wall, like spots on a giraffe. Real trees surrounded the wall, but those trees sat back a bit as though to make sure the wall had a view out over the clearing.

A door split the wall in half. Or perhaps it was a gate. Sasha and Toddy had never seen anything like it. It was metal and tugged at its huge rusted hinges as if it were heavy. At the top it arched and at the bottom it was straight. The metal was shaped into limbs and branches and vines and leaves, and all those shapes swirled together to create a whole garden within the four feet wide and six feet tall of the gate. As Sasha studied the gate, flowers—so many different and beautiful kinds, like red roses and white gardenias and purple clematis—appeared and disappeared as she turned her head left to right.

"Should we knock?" Sasha asked her brother.

Toddy tried to peek in between the vines to see what lay beyond, but as he did, the vines pushed together to obstruct his view. He turned to Sasha with bright, wide-awake eyes and a grin that grew larger by the second.

"Let's go in," he said.

Sasha raised her hand to tap on a burnished copper leaf, but before she could knock, the gate swung slowly on its hinges, just wide enough for the two of them to slip through. The gate shut again behind them with a gentle clink.

They strained to see more than a few feet in front of them once they had gotten past the gate. Flora grew robustly all around, nearly taking over the narrow pebble path they stood on.

From over their heads a weeping cherry tree with luscious pink blossoms tapped their shoulders in welcome. Silver moonlight filtered through the tree, and

Sasha and Toddy were suddenly hungry for Madam Mermadia's fairy floss. Orderly daffodils lined the path on one side. When Toddy walked by, they turned their trumpet faces to him and giggled. On the other side of the path, stately tulips in a rainbow of colors swayed to tinkling music that Sasha could just barely hear. Ferns waved greetings with pebbled frond-fingers, and flowers with petals like drooping dogs' tongues licked their legs as they strolled by.

Sasha caught a glimpse of light between two clumps of leaves. "Toddy, look."

The brother and sister crowded close to peer at the place beyond the garden. There was a structure of some sort—a house maybe, but they could only see a roof—and beyond that . . .

Nothing. No garden. No sea. No sky. Just white light.

"We made it," Sasha said. "The Edge of the World."

Sasha and Toddy walked on, meeting each new flower or tree with wondering smiles. How could this place of beauty possibly be the home of a bitter, scheming Magician? They grasped their hands together and walked along the path, pausing as a playful troupe of tiny purple-and-red frogs leaped across the path in front of them. Pirate chased those frogs, until one landed on his nose and stared the kitten down fiercely. Then it leaped off again and Pirate kept his paws to himself.

Soon enough the three garden visitors reached that small building they'd seen through the leaves. The front was lined with a long white porch, like a sweet cottage from an old story. Sasha and Toddy climbed the three steps and stood before the front door. A brass plate on the pale blue door was blank.

"Don't those usually say who lives in a house?" Sasha wondered. She knocked on the door. No one answered.

"Should we go in?" Toddy said.

Sasha squinted at the shimmering brass plate, sure she'd seen the beginnings of letters appear. The next moment, though, it was blank again.

"Don't you think we'll be in trouble if this is someone's house?" But even as she asked, she was thinking that it would be very nice to sleep with a roof over their heads, although it might be even nicer to sleep under the popcorn fingers of the weeping cherry tree.

Sasha raised her hand to knock again, but this time the door swung open before she could make contact with her knuckles.

On that brass plate the words finally made themselves clear: THE MAGICIAN. ENTER AT YOUR OWN RISK.

CHAPTER 29

Shadows lurked in corners, and glitter-dust swirled in the moonlight shining through the building's highest windows. Sasha took a hesitant step over the threshold. "Hello?"

No answer greeted them. Sasha pulled Toddy in behind her. They walked carefully across the smooth, wooden floor, their shoes whispering as they scuffed. The room was large and lined in stones. The ceiling was covered with dark tiles shimmering like obsidian. Sasha marveled at the difference between the size of the house from the outside and the size of it—though it seemed more like a castle than a house in there—from the inside. Great iron sconces lit the room and the hallways that snaked away to their left and right.

Sasha's second "Hello" echoed twice before it disappeared into the dark angles of stone. Even more of a contrast was the dark chill that weighed over her shoulders. All the joy of the gardens was dashed from Sasha's mind and heart. She felt heavy here. And so terribly sad.

"Do you think this is the Magician's home?" Toddy said.

"I think this is it," Sasha said. "If the Unimoose was right." She looked left to right, squinting in the hopes that the right hallway, the one they should take to find the Magician, would be revealed. "Which way should we go?"

Toddy's little body shuddered. "Home. I don't like it here. There are things floating in the air. Like ghosts. Don't they scare you?"

Sasha looked all around, but the only thing she saw was the flickering of low yellow light against the walls. She almost told her brother that maybe he was imagining things, but once she got a good, long look at his ashen face, she bit her tongue. Pirate huddled in Toddy's arms, his eyes as round as full moons.

"It'll be okay," she said, but even she didn't entirely believe herself. Her voice wobbled and she too wanted nothing more than to go home. Instead she nodded her chin to the right. "Let's go this way."

"I miss Daddy and Mommy," Toddy said.

"Me too."

Sasha missed the still, silent nights they'd spent together in quiet work, reading books or finishing costumes. She missed watching Mom twirl around the ribbons during practice and helping Dad perfect his own flips and twists. She missed hugs and smiles and patience and laughter. She missed the loud, boisterous nights when they invited their friends into their home and everyone told a story about a strange and wonderful place they'd seen when they were younger.

For Mom it was always the trail she'd taken across plains and over mountains to reach the Cirque. She'd come upon a meadow teeming with lilac and butterflies during that journey, and she'd stopped there to sleep. She'd dreamed of her future that night, seeing the Cirque and her husband-to-be and her years growing old with her friends and children surrounding her. And now Sasha held the realization of that dream in her own palm. If she didn't find Mom and Dad, it would never come true.

Toddy interrupted Sasha's thoughts with a tight squeeze of her hand. "I'm glad you love me."

They walked down the hallway, Toddy and Pirate still shivering beside Sasha. Every minute or two Toddy would jump or duck or hide behind his sister. There was something going on in his mind—or in front of his eyes—that she couldn't be part of, no matter how much she wanted to help him. She walked faster, hoping to leave Toddy's ghosts behind. She wanted so much to help him be less scared. Her fists clenched. How frustrating it was to be so helpless!

The walls began changing. First they took on pale rainbow hues; then the rainbows changed to wooden squares with little circles in the center. Sasha went closer to explore. What she had thought was wallpaper turned out to be hundreds of small, square drawers set into the stone, each with a different knob.

There was a strong desire to open the drawers. To let the huge manor house reveal its secrets. But what if the drawers contained horrors? Sasha brushed her fear aside and reached her fingers to the drawer directly in front of her, at chest height. She pulled.

Joyful music filled the room. Lights flickered and danced. Inside the drawer the tiny Cirque was entertaining thousands of tourists. There were gasps of delight and giggles. Drumrolls and grinning acrobats. It was Sasha's world. Her favorite place. Every unhappy part of her vanished as she watched. Until a darkness began to settle over the scene. Sasha's shoulders tightened and her neck ached. Smoke rolled in, covering everyone and everything until the tent became ashes and the performers became skeletons.

Sasha slammed the drawer closed. Her heart beat

madly. Was that the future she'd ushered in? Death and destruction for the Cirque? She backed away from the wall quickly, searching for Toddy.

"Where are you?"

"It's terrible," his little voice said. It came from under a table. "The creatures are everywhere and they won't show me their faces."

Sasha gathered her brother and looked around the room. She couldn't decide where to go next, especially when she didn't want to go anywhere else. Every time she thought she was brave, something proved her wrong. The Magician was terribly scary.

But her dad's voice echoed in her mind. *You know what's scary? Opening yourself up to others to love with all your heart.* Sasha knew she couldn't give all her heart to love if so much of it was filled with fear.

"We must go on, Toddy. I think . . ." Sasha raised her arm and pointed. "We should go that way."

CHAPTER 30

They moved toward the corner Sasha had pointed to. A soft light grew as they approached, illuminating a long hallway. It must have been a trick of the eyes, but the hallway seemed to go on forever and ever. The walls were covered with painted scenes of all kinds, from pastoral baby animals and spring breezes, to deeply colored swirls and stars in purples, yellows, and silver.

Doors were set in between the murals, each one a different color and each doorknob a different style. There was a bright red door with a long, black iron handle; a tall metal door decorated with knights riding horses and princesses waiting in tall castle turrets; and even a door painted to look like a slab cut right out of the middle of a tree with a little hole drilled in it, out of which hung a rope latch.

After they had passed a dozen doors at least, they stopped at a cream-colored door with an old-fashioned cut-crystal and brass knob.

"This one's pretty." Sasha grasped the cool knob in her hand, turned it until it clicked, and pushed the door open. All the air in the hallway seemed to rush like eager fairies into the room, blowing Sasha's dress in a whirlwind around her body.

The room was big—bigger than their whole cottage back home. At the far wall across from the door was a window taller and wider than an elephant, covered with layers of filmy silk drapes.

The furniture in the room was white, buffed with age at the corners, with brass knobs in the shapes of exotic animals, some of which Sasha had never seen before and had no names for. Others were familiar: the Unimoose, the Sharp-Beaked Weasel. Even—

"Pirate!" Toddy called the kitten over to compare him to the knob. They had the same striped tail, the same pointy ears, and even the same eyes: one open, one forever closed.

Pirate was unimpressed. He hissed at the knob.

The bed itself was a great big thing right in the middle of the room, made of tall, swirling brass posts.

Over the top and down the sides of the bed draped long white curtains that ended in puddles of fabric on the floor. The top of the bed was so high that there was a little set of stairs to climb up on. The fluffy white duvet was embroidered with colorful train sets, dolls sitting to tea, cuddly teddy bears, and beribboned ponies. The pillows looked as soft and fluffy as cotton-ball clouds.

Sasha hesitated. The Islanders called her dirty. She didn't want to spoil the room. But Toddy took her hand, and they stepped over a set of wooden blocks that had tumbled out onto the floor, walked around the rocking horse with its brown yarn mane, and lay across the middle of the bed. They immediately sank three inches down with a contented sigh.

"It's the fluffiest thing ever." Sasha rubbed her fists in her eyes. She could stay there forever. The bed was so comfortable and she was so tired . . . but that window! What could be outside that window?

Sasha bit her lip, then rushed to the window for just one peek, brushing the curtain aside and sneaking between it and the cool glass beyond. Light like morning brightened the outdoors, and the sky looked like an iridescent marble, swirling with pearly colors. She looked down and there seemed to be no ground out there, beyond the window. It was as though the Magician's home were perched on the side of a hill, the stone foundation hanging onto their world for dear life.

She caught sight of a shadow flitting by, then another one. "Birds," Sasha breathed. "Mom? Dad?"

Her eyes searched for their familiar feathers until they watered. She refused to blink, refused to look away, in case she missed her mom and dad flying by. There was a way to open the window. A latch at the lowest part, pulled to the side, would let Sasha push the glass away and step out to the forest world. Sasha desperately wanted to swing that latch and step outside. She would hold Toddy's hand and they would join the birds—be with her parents again—flying away into the expanse of pines. She went so far as to bend over, reach her fingers to the metal, and grip it. Just one sharp movement, and she could leave this world behind.

"Sasha?" Toddy's voice from the bed was so small compared to the big world outside the window.

She forced herself to turn away from the glass and look at him.

"What are you doing?"

"They must be out there," Sasha said.

But when Sasha looked out the window once more, the birds were gone. The sky was dark. And all that lay below the window was a maw of shadows. Sasha's heart gave a sudden leap in her chest, reminding her that this place didn't belong to her and that magicians could be deceitful. Of course the Magician wanted her to enter the world outside the window. The fall would destroy her. It would keep her away from him forever.

Sasha splayed her fingers over the glass. "Once, I wanted to become a fish and swim away," she said to herself. "Change, just like Mom and Dad did and go far away where no one could find me. Free in a new world, instead of stuck in the one with the Islanders. But maybe I'm not stuck. The Cirque is so beautiful. The Magician must miss it." Sasha's eyes widened. "Maybe *he's* stuck in here. In this terrible place of ghosts and Smoke."

She pulled her hand away, scrunched her eyes, and pinched her mouth, then relaxed her muscles and let out a sigh.

When she turned around, all the furniture in the room except the bed had disappeared, and there was a new set of curtains behind her. Sasha wrinkled her eyebrows. She knew they hadn't been there when she'd first entered the room. These curtains, though, weren't light, shimmering things but heavy drapes, dropping from the ceiling in the center of the room and puddling at the floor. There was no feeling that Sasha should go to *these* curtains; instead her stomach hurt, as a ball of dread sank to the bottom of her belly.

She wanted to run. Turn and run all the way home,

without her parents, without Toddy and Pirate, even, who both slept gently on the fluffy bed.

Sasha faced the bedroom door, prepared to flee. Her heart raced with fear.

The room went deathly silent. Then there was a soft, high sound, like laughter but very far away.

"Who's there?" Sasha whispered.

A zephyr blew the curtains. Sasha approached. It was difficult to move, as though a force pushed against her body, warning her not to come closer. Sasha hesitated, biting her lip. It could be dangerous to look behind these curtains, she knew. But there was a little piece of her . . . something deep in her heart . . . that made her feel like she had to keep going. She reached a tentative finger toward the curtains. They stilled. The soft laughter changed to a low growl. A warning.

"You can't scare me." Her voice trembled. Her lip ached where her teeth pressed down on it.

"Are you sure? I think I already have. Go back, little girl. Live forever with the Unimoose. No one would miss you."

There *was* someone there. Its voice was smug and sure, and the arrogance of the words made Sasha furious. The owner of that voice didn't know her heart; they couldn't gauge her bravery. She had come this far, and she wasn't backing down now. The Smoke must be defeated.

With a rush Sasha flung aside the curtains.

Behind them stood a tall mirror.

"It would have been easier for everyone if you'd chosen my way. But come inside, girl, if you must. If terror and sadness is what you crave."

Yes, that was what Sasha had to do. Face the Magician in the mirror. Face his terror and sadness.

Face herself.

She gazed in the mirror for a long time, long enough that her eyes took on a new depth and her jaw a new set of determination. Her shoulders rounded back with deeper strength.

Sasha stepped through the glass.

CHAPTER 31

A Cirque world swirled around her. She was inside a dark tent, lit by spinning neon colors. Glitter and sparkles and strobe lights confused her. All around, Cirque performers twisted and flipped, coming close to Sasha to wave their hands near her head and make grotesque faces, before dissolving into the shadows again. Above, hoops and tightrope lines were packed with skeletal figures; every few seconds one of them crashed to the ground and disappeared. Just like her dad. Everywhere, there was tin-can music and hideous laughter.

Sasha closed her eyes and swallowed back sobs. She wanted to go home.

"Go, then. You don't belong here. But do you belong anywhere? Why should Cirque Magnifique take you back when you said you hated them?"

A finger tucked under Sasha's chin and tipped her face up. She opened her eyes. Before her, a tall figure encased in sweeping robes gazed down at her. His eyes were like Toddy's: full of the universe. But where Toddy's were beautiful and wondrous, the Magician's were full of the fear of endlessness, of being lost and never found, of being forgotten. Of being able to see into every shadow and corner of her feelings.

He looked exactly like the drawing she'd seen in Mr. Ticklefar's book of Cirque lore.

He terrified her.

The neon colors faded, and all movement stopped. Smoke rose from the ground, obscuring Sasha's feet and ankles.

"Or you can stay here." The Magician dropped her chin and turned in a slow circle. "All the wonders of eternity can be yours. Spend your days in the most beautiful garden you've ever seen and your nights blowing plumes of Smoke across the earth. Marvel at wonders no other humans know of. Abandon fear and be in peace forever."

It sounded too good to be true. Too lovely, too easy. Sasha wanted to fall into the Magician's world and never have to worry again. Never be bullied again, never have her heart broken again.

"We could be happy here . . . ," she began. The Magician cut her off.

"We?"

"Me and Toddy and Mom and Dad and Pirate."

"Little girl, there is no Toddy and Mom and Dad and Pirate. You came in here alone. Refusing help, as you always do. You want to leave everything behind, don't you? Stay here forever."

Sasha looked over her shoulder, as though Toddy would be there. He was always there. But not this time. It felt awful to be alone.

Her legs still ached from all the walking she'd done; her hands were still scratched from the Grandelion; her hair still smelled like salt water from battling King Crab. And always, always, her heart ached with the way the Islanders called her names.

But when she was with her family at the Cirque, surrounded by her friends . . .

"The garden is lovely . . ."

"Yes. Very lovely." The Magician beckoned with his hands. "You want to stay."

"But it's loveliest at home. When the sky is clear and the air smells like the sea and the cedars whisper. Even when the sky is gray and the waves slam the shore and the winds howl." Sasha tilted her head, understanding why the Magician wanted her to stay at the Edge of the World. She spoke softly. "The only time the Cirque isn't beautiful is when the Smoke covers everything and makes us afraid. You want me to stay so that I can't defeat you. So you can keep bullying the Cirque forever. Well . . . I won't let you."

The Magician floated and twirled above her, his face dark with anger.

"Nonsense. That island is dark and dreary. The Islanders despise you, and the Cirque blames you for bringing back the Smoke. It is not the loveliest. It *cannot* be the loveliest. There is no such thing as love. It is an illusion."

"That's not true!" Sasha dug her fists into her hips. "There is love. And the Cirque doesn't blame me. No, they blame *you*, you dastardly, devilish Magician, for creating the Smoke in the first place!"

The Magician waved his arms. The room filled with Smoke until Sasha couldn't see through it. Then, with one great blow of his breath, the Magician cleared the Smoke away again.

"The Smoke is always there. Only you decide if you want it or not." The Magician lowered to the ground. His face, still so young-looking, went as cold as ice. "If you don't take my offer, I will destroy you." The Magician said the terrible words matter-of-factly.

"Destroy me? That's awful!"

"Didn't you come here to destroy me? Turnabout is fair play."

"Yes—I mean . . . no, actually. I don't want to destroy *you,* though I feel terribly sorry for you. I came to destroy the Smoke. I came to find my parents, to keep Toddy with me, to rescue Cirque Magnifique!"

"You are too scared and alone to rescue anyone."

Sasha wanted to scream *No!* but she didn't. She held her tongue. Fear, after all, was something she'd struggled with on this entire journey: fear of sailing out to sea, fear of not being able to save Toddy from King Crab or the Sharp-Beaked Weasel. Fear of never seeing her parents again. Pushing through that fear had been one of the most wonderful things Sasha had ever done in her life. Even now, the chance to leave the world behind was like a wrapped gift in her hands, and all she had to do was pull the ribbon off.

She thought of all the things on the island that made her fearful.

Then she thought of all the things that made her happy. And all the bravery she'd seen. Her mom and dad soaring through the air when they performed at the Cirque. Toddy following her to the Edge of the World. Even Pirate, learning to trust Toddy after the other kids treated the kitten so badly. The Cirque was a community; it was family.

"I'm not scared and I'm not alone," Sasha said. "I never have been."

"Your fear shines like light off a mirror. You want to hurt the people who have hurt you."

Sasha knew the Magician didn't speak the truth. And that's when the truth found Sasha, like a bird calling out to her across a dense forest. It was something her dad had said to her:

Love always makes us better than we were before. It makes Lights of us all.

In that moment Sasha's emotions shone like a light off a mirror, which meant . . .

Cirque lore had been wrong about the Light. It wasn't some special magic that kept the Smoke at bay. Something that only one person at a time could carry. The magic, Light, was something they *all* had, if only they were brave enough to love mightily. It was they, themselves. Not Lights, in fact. . . . They were *Mirrors*, and all the good of their hearts could be reflected into the world. If only they knew they had the power. If only they didn't always shrink from the Magician and his Smoke, and instead gathered their strength and fought it off, like Griffin had always said they should.

Sasha took a deep breath. She searched her mind and her heart and gathered all the love, all the bravery, all the power she held there. She remembered every game of hide-and-seek played around the Cirque tents. She thought about all the smiles the performers sent her way as they walked past, dazzling her with their flamboyant costumes. She recalled every storytelling night in the cottage, when her dad told the story about when Mom walked into the Cirque.

The Cirque was a wonderful place to be. They were strong, together. And now she would show the Magician how tough she was, how her magic was, indeed, enough. How *she* was enough—good enough—no matter what anyone said or did to her. With her eyes closed she pushed all those good memories toward the Magician. She became a Mirror.

She never saw the way her light blasted the neon and the strange performers, or how the Smoke dissipated forever, or how the Magician curled his lip and tried to hide from all that beamed from Sasha. She only listened to his wail fade into nothingness as the dark thoughts in her soul were replaced with a sweet longing for her family. And when that sound was gone, Sasha crumpled to the ground, spent.

CHAPTER 32

Toddy rolled over and sighed at the stream of light trickling across the bed. "Sasha," he said. "I don't want to be here anymore. I want to go home today."

"Today?" Confusion blanketed Sasha's mind like a soft rain.

She sat up in the bed, where she was tucked next to her brother, and looked around the room. The furniture had returned and the mirror was gone. There was a bright feeling in her chest. What had happened after she'd sent the Smoke away? She was sure she had been caught in the Magician's world so much longer than just a night.

A gentle breeze ruffled her short, uneven locks, and she looked to the window.

"Toddy. It's open!"

Sasha and Toddy tossed the blankets aside and ran to the window. It was pushed wide, letting a crisp, citrus scent fill the room. The garden was alive with the delightful chirping of birds and rattling of leaves. Sasha wanted to walk out and join the fun, but she looked down to be reminded that they were dozens of feet above the ground. Just as Sasha was wishing she and Toddy had wings, two huge birds darted across her line of vision. A black raptor with bands of white at its shoulders, and a vibrantly colored tropical bird sporting all the colors of a jungle rain forest. They disappeared into the far trees, then circled back to land on a branch just beyond the reach of the children. The raptor snapped its beak at them.

"Dad! Oh, you *were* the sea eagle on the hill. And, Mom, you distracted King Crab. You were with us the whole time." Sasha's giggle soared between the vines tracking up the tree trunks, and the clematis blossoms tittered back.

Sasha took her brother's hand. She raised her foot and leaned forward into the breeze, knowing it would catch her first step, and the second and third, until she was racing away lightly, dancing on the wind.

A rush of air met them, drawing them from the world of the manor and the room completely, ruffling the edges of their clothing. The black bird and the colorful bird soared close by. Toddy called to her. He darted quickly to and fro, his tiny feathers green and gold like a hummingbird's. Sasha slowly flapped her long, red-of-a-million-shades wings and sang back.

They sailed over the treetops and climbed into the cloud-laden sky with shrieks of laughter. They raced through the day and into the night, pausing to dangle off the tip of the crescent moon for a moment, looking at the earth far, far below, before soaring silently into the inky blackness and the shimmering stars beyond. And when they tired, they headed for a dark speck against a backdrop of deepest blue. A place where sequins glittered and flags flapped in a salty ocean breeze.

It was time to go home.

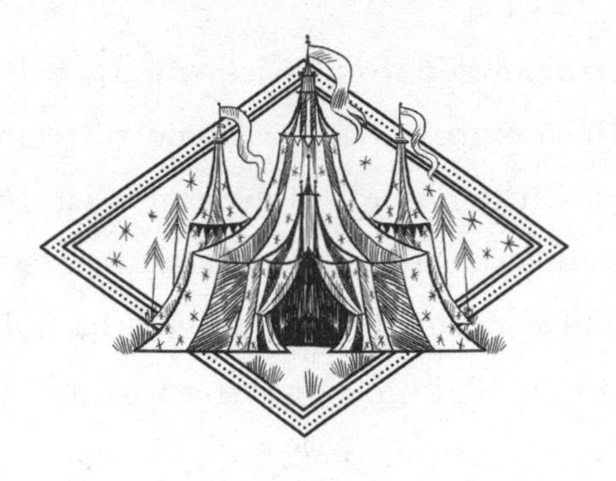

CHAPTER 33

There would still be gray skies greeting the cars coming over the hill to see the storied Cirque Magnifique. There had to be gray, to remind Sasha that some days and nights were meant for cozy storytelling in the cottage. And there had to be gray so that when the skies were clear blue she was dazzled by their perfection. On one of those cloudless days, Jenny Myers came over from the other side of the island.

"I've been waiting for you to come back," she said. "Kirk and Colton and all those boys said I was stupid to wait and that you were never coming back. None of you were. But you're here, and they're . . . well, they're stuck in their own awfulness."

Jenny sat on the ground with her legs crossed, as

though she belonged to the Cirque and always had. She watched the contortionists practice on outdoor mats and squinted when their rhinestones caught the sun and sent its rays streaming toward her in a light brighter than she had ever seen before. She let out a slow breath.

"There is something about the Cirque," Jenny said. "I don't know how to explain it."

It was something compelling. There always had been a pull to the Cirque side of the island for Jenny, ever since that first time she'd escaped from Gran's house and went walking along a deer path, her legs seeming to know exactly where to go even though her mind didn't. Gran had found her on the edge of the Cirque and hauled her back home, and it was after that that Gran started telling Jenny stories of the terrible and frightening things that happened to Cirque folks. *You are never to set foot on that side of the island,* Gran had told her. *Do you want to disappear into Smoke someday too?*

And yet here she was, tucked in like she had always been part of the Cirque, eager to hear Sasha's tales.

"You invited me to your birthday party," Sasha said.

Jenny nibbled on a fingernail. "I did it kind of . . . secretly. I wish I hadn't. I wish I'd been braver. Then you'd have known that I didn't hate you. I'm sorry," Jenny continued. Now she looked up at Sasha, as though seeing her for the first time. "I wasn't very nice to you. I didn't think

I was supposed to be. Isn't that strange? Why would someone *want* me to be mean? But I was, and I'm really sorry."

Mr. Ticklefar, walking past the cottages to check on everyone as he was wont to do in the afternoons, overheard Jenny Myers and paused.

"You're Mable Thompson's granddaughter, then? Me and yer gran knew each other very well, once upon a time. She was a fine girl and loved to hear my travelin' stories. I asked her to come here. To stay." Mr. Ticklefar got a faraway look on his face. He adjusted his top hat so that it sat a little more to the side than the center, and he ran his hand over his beard. "She wouldn't come. Said I should go to her side of the island, but I was just as stubborn as she was, and if she wouldn't come here, well, I wasn't going over there! We quarreled long and hard. I guess you could say we're still quarreling to this day, since we haven't spoken all these years. My heart ain't very hard no more, and I wish her well. Always did, really. Her and her little ones. I kept a bit of an eye on you. Just one eye, mind."

Mr. Ticklefar laughed and pointed to his eye patch. "I remember the day you came waddling to our side of the island. You mighta been about two. Chubby legs and big eyes. That was the last time I saw you, though. 'Cept for now. Don't know how you convinced your gran to let you come over."

"I didn't," Jenny said. "She's taking her nap and I just came. I *had* to. It itched at me, staying away all this time."

Sasha's mom looked up from the costume she was adorning with lavender lace. "I know a bit about that feeling," she said absently. "It's not a thing you can fight forever."

"Some of us were just meant to be here," Mr. Ticklefar said. "It's that kind of a place, Cirque Magnifique."

The ringmaster looked up as Griffin passed by, carrying a box of heavy stage lights. Mr. Ticklefar nodded in the boy's direction. "Even he's meant to be here. He knows it, and I know it."

Sasha frowned. "I still don't think he believes in any of it: the Magician and Smoke and Mirrors."

"Does he have to?" Mr. Ticklefar asked. "He's got a good talent for what he does and he enjoys it and he's part of our commun'ty. So he's got a few friends on the other side, what of it? Bet no one e'er told you 'bout the time he shouted down an Islander boy for teasin' his sister, did they? He's a Mirror of his own sort. Always has been. Anyway, it ain't our belief in stories that makes us what we are. It's our belief in one another. And he's got that in spades, even if he's got a diff'rent way of showing it."

Mr. Ticklefar continued on his walk, and Sasha pulled her own costume into her lap and picked up her needle and thread. She hadn't told anyone that she was ready to return to her role in the Cirque. She didn't have to. Her bravery had shown them. While she added beads to her tulle skirt, she told Jenny about pirate ships that sprouted from marble-like rain forest seeds, and moose with silver heads and rainbow horns.

The two would work through old hurts in the coming weeks and, in leaps and bounds as children often could manage, become best friends.

It would even change things at school.

"Toddy! Sasha!" Miss Islip flew down the hallway the moment the brother and sister stepped foot through the school door. The teacher gathered them up, then pulled back and searched their faces. Whatever she saw there made a smile push her rosy cheeks right up to her eyes. "This old place hasn't been the same without you."

"We didn't think you'd be here still," Sasha said.

"I'll be here some time longer. Mrs. Flint decided to stay in Florida for good. She realized how much she hated the gray skies, but I think she just had a hard time seeing the way the sun shines through the folds of sky in between the clouds."

Sasha left Toddy in Miss Islip's classroom and walked to her own. It didn't take long to get there. Just down the hall and around the corner. Odd, Sasha thought, how long the walk used to take. Many, many minutes, before she'd banished the Smoke. But this day it was only a moment, and a sweet one, as Jenny Myers joined her halfway so they could enter the classroom together.

Kirk Stoddard still sat behind Sasha's desk. His hands were folded in front of him and he stared straight ahead. Sasha paused. Watched him. If they were all Mirrors, then Kirk Stoddard reflected only the meanest, saddest things possible. And that made Sasha feel sorry for him. When he finally looked up at her, he flinched. *Her* Mirror was exceptionally lovely. He didn't deserve the kindness of Sasha's reflection, exactly, and Sasha was confused by her own actions for a long time—why treat him so well when he had been so awful to her?—but she did it anyway. And it felt good.

Kirk Stoddard would never speak to Sasha again. He never said sorry, but he never said terrible things either. He simply looked away from her, as though her brilliance were too great for him to bear.

Jenny, however, was a faithful friend to Sasha at school and at the Cirque, on those days she could slip away from Gran's watchful eye. One day Jenny would join the Cirque and stay with Sasha forever, exclaiming over the stories Sasha told. Toddy, as always when Sasha told her long-winded tales, would say nothing. He'd only watch Mr. Ticklefar with his big, universe-filled eyes as the ringmaster ordered about the Cirque performers and dreamed up new ways to use the light of their Mirrors in the shows, and pet Pirate, who had grown up to be a very good mouser and explorer in his own right.

For when Sasha and Toddy and Mom and Dad returned to the island, they told the performers about Mirrors. How they all were reflections of love and kindness. How every single one of them was in possession of a Mirror, not just a select few.

"You do it like this," Sasha said when the entire Cirque was gathered in the big tent, watching Sasha with wonder in their eyes. Mr. Ticklefar, twirling his mustache. Aunt Chanteuse, ready to write a new song about Sasha's adventures. The triplets, their golden-foil wigs glinting under the lights. Madame Mermadia, trailing sparkles from the tips of her hair. Shelby and Griffin, whose own teasing for being Cirque kids had come to a stop. Mom and Dad, beaming up at her.

They couldn't stop looking at the light that radiated from her entire body. Sasha was nervous, having to teach something she didn't entirely understand herself, but everyone was so eager and warm that their Mirrors were already starting to form and reflect back at her.

"You . . ." Sasha paused. Closed her eyes. "You remember every nice thing that's happened to you. The people who hugged you when you were sad. The ones who invited you to their birthday party and gave you the nicest piece of cake. You think about the most beautiful sights on the island. The deer trail in the morning when it's still damp and quiet and all the animals are nosing about in the ferns. Or that time you went tidepooling on Anders' Rock and got stranded by the high tide so long that you saw the hundreds of colors of the sunset. You giggle at the funniest joke you've ever heard, the one that's been your favorite since you were five, and you remember a song that you just *have* to dance to, and then . . . what you do is . . ."

Sasha opened her eyes. The big tent quivered with anticipation.

"You wish all that love and beauty and fun and wonder for everyone around you. You give it. Like a gift."

Sasha held her hands in front of her. All the Cirque folk copied her, and as one they shined their light for all to see. On the other side of the island, people glanced out their windows and wondered if a strange celestial event were occurring. A meteor blazing into the atmosphere, or a solar eclipse brightening the sky with a strange, golden light at a too-late hour of the evening. What they didn't know was that a little girl was near-to-bursting with a joy that would shame the sun itself.

And that joy, above all other things, kept the Cirque safe and happy.

The Edge of the World

The Magician walked through his castle slowly, as he had every moment since waking from the strange dream of a little girl. Had it even been a dream? His brain felt muddled. A magic trick gone wrong?

His robes swirled around his ankles, and the bag of tricks tied to his waist clicked and clinked. The shadows kept him company, as they had for hundreds of years. The Smoke, though . . .

He reached out his fingers. They stubbornly refused to call up the Smoke. It had been banished somehow. Strangely, the Magician hardly missed it.

He left the castle and stepped through the garden he had planted for Lilit. The one she had never seen. At the Magician's approach, the birds silenced their songs and the frogs hid under big, glossy leaves, watching the ageless man warily until he had passed through the gate, before recommencing their leaping game.

The Magician walked all the way to the sea.

"You always haunted my dreams," he said to the blustery wind. "You always teased me mercilessly," he said to the foam-tipped waves lapping at his boots.

He looked to the south, where many days before, four beautiful birds had vanished from his world forever. Then he looked to the north.

A ripple in the sea caught his attention. The breeze blew his hat from his head, but he let it roll down the beach and out of sight. A huge black-and-white whale rose from the water, breaching grandly, then fell back again with a mighty splash.

"But you . . . you were always clear about what you did and didn't want. And I refused to listen."

The Magician waded farther into the sea and wished with all his heart to change into the same creature as her, just as he had wished every month since the day he'd vanished to the Edge of the World. But this pilgrimage ended like all the others: with the waves increasing and rising, pushing him back to the shore, lest he be drowned by them.

For the first time the Magician did not swell with bitterness and anger.

"I only ever wanted to change too," he mused.

The image of a stubborn little girl and a steady little boy flickered in his mind. He'd forgotten what hope looked like. Forgotten how magic could bring joy, until seeing them in his castle. But memories, even ones that had slept so deeply and for so long, never really disappeared. Forgetting was an illusion. The greatest trick of all. But remembering . . . that was real. The first smile in hundreds of years played across his features.

"And so I have changed."

The wind giggled and tickled his ears. The Magician spread his arms. The transition was sudden: a shocking weightlessness, and the wind pulled him off his feet. He flapped his white wings several times to practice, clacked his big orange beak, and flew off to the east to find his next adventure.

ACKNOWLEDGMENTS

My sincerest thanks to the brilliant minds and skills of those who helped make this book a reality, in particular:

My truly insightful editor, Sylvie Frank; publisher, Paula Wiseman; managing editor, Jenica Nasworthy; art director, Chloë Foglia; assistant editor, Sarah Jane Abbott; copy editor, Bara MacNeill; and production manager, Chava Wolin; as well as the rest of the fabulous team at Paula Wiseman Books and Simon & Schuster. My thanks and admiration to Karl James Mountford for the gorgeous cover and interior illustrations.

Brent Taylor, agent extraordinaire and champion of words, and Uwe Stender and the team at TriadaUS.

My bogiest of besties: thank you for being the greatest of friends and colleagues.

Last in these words, but first in my heart, always and forever: Aidyn, Aine, Arran, and Paul.